"Skeletons In The Closet"

(Edited By Logan Bruce)

Published by The ORB
www.orb-store.com

Copyright © Studio NI 2013
All rights reserved. No part of this publication may be reproduced, stored in a retrieval system or transmitted in any form or by any means electronic, mechanical, photocopying, recording or otherwise, without the prior written permission of the author.

Stories:
Sentenced	Copyright © Amanda Finch 2013
Irish Roots	Copyright © Gerry McCullough 2013
The Man Code	Copyright © Conor Mc Varnock 2013
Garantan	Copyright © Holly Ferres 2013
Souvenirs	Copyright ©Lynda Collins 2013
The Spirit: A Tale of Misdirection	Copyright © Ellie Rose McKee 2013
Unsolved	Copyright ©Ellie Rose McKee 2013
McGinty, Armchair Detective	Copyright © Logan Bruce 2013
In the Closet?	Copyright © Logan Bruce 2013
Who Burned Billizabeth?	Copyright © Logan Bruce 2013

Illustrations:
Cover photograph	Copyright © Ellie Rose McKee 2013
Line-up	Copyright ©Lynda Collins 2013
Skeletons in the Closet	Copyright © Logan Bruce 2013

Profits to Charity pledge

For every copy of this book sold, one pound (20%) of the cover price will go to the charity nominated by Studio NI, the largest Arts and Culture Group in the North of Ireland.

At time of publication, the nominated charity is
Action Cancer (Charity reg no. XN 48533)

Index

4	**Introduction**	
5	**Sentenced**	*Amanda Finch*
15	**Irish Roots**	*Gerry McCullough*
25	**The Man Code**	*Conor Mc Varnock*
39	**Garantan**	*Holly Ferres*
53	**Souvenirs**	*Lynda Collins*
62	**Line-Up** (illustration)	*Lynda Collins*
63	**The Spirit: A Tale of Misdirection**	*Ellie Rose McKee*
73	**Unsolved**	*Ellie Rose McKee*
83	**McGinty, Armchair Detective**	*Logan Bruce*
93	**In the Closet?**	*Logan Bruce*
100	**Who Burned Billizabeth?**	*Logan Bruce*
112	**Skeletons in the Closet** (illustration)	*Logan Bruce*
113	**TITANIA 2013 Poetry Entries**	
131	**TitanFest 2013 Awards Ceremony Weekend Booklet**	

Introduction

Every year, Studio NI holds the TITANIA contests - the Top Independent Talented Artistes N.I. Awards. These contests are open to all persons holding an annual VIP membership of Studio NI. They take place during the "Titans of Ulster" Festival, a 4-month event that is supported by the Arts Council of Northern Ireland. The 2013 Awards are sponsored by Waterstones, No Alibis Books and Blackstaff Press.

The theme for entries in the 2013 contest is: "Skeletons in the Closet". This theme was chosen specifically with the TITANIA contest in mind, because it is an indirect reference to a certain title by Belfast-born writer CS Lewis. The "Titans Of Ulster" Festival's 2013 Awards Ceremony weekend takes place on the 50th anniversary of Lewis' death, so the two events are synonymous.

The Celebrity Author judges on the 2013 shortlisting panel include International best-selling Crime/Mystery novelist John Connolly and Hugo Award-winning Science Fiction writer Ian McDonald. The shortlisted works from the TITANIA 2013 short story contest are collated in this anthology, published by Studio NI to raise funds for the Curing Cancer campaign. Also included are a selection of Public Domain poems that were included in the TITANIA 2013 music & poetry video contest shortlist, to be shown in association with Foyle Film Festival.

The anthology "Skeletons in the Closet" will be launched at the "Titans of Ulster" Festival in Autumn 2013 - and for every copy of this book that is sold, £1 goes to Action Cancer. The vote for the winner of the TITANIA will be concluded at next year's "Titans of Ulster" Festival in Autumn 2014.

To vote for your choice in the TITANIA contest, visit www.TitanFest.com

Sentenced
Amanda Finch

The first drop hits the Y key. It lies there, dark and viscous in the slight dip that is meant for my fingertip, obscuring the letter.
    The second drop falls on the O. The letter holds it for a moment, an imperfect circle, then the weight of the globule overspills the white line.
    U. The third drop smashes down, obliterating the letter and spattering the whole keyboard.

* * *

I wake panting, shaking. It's ok. It's all ok. I'm in my own bed in my own room at home. There is no one here. There are no letters. No keyboards. No computers. I lie very still, as still as I can, staring at the ceiling, waiting for the blood to clear from my mind. I'm still shivering and the old springs in the bed keep up a low whining vibration no matter how hard I try to stop them. It's creepy as. I wish Mum would cough up and get me a new bed like any normal parent. This one is doing my head in. I squeeze my hands together, press my back into the bed and curl my toes. I can control this. It's pathetic being scared of a dream. I'll just forget it. I will. Slowly, the bed stops groaning and I realise that means I've stopped shaking.
    It is taking longer every night.
    YOU
    Just YOU these last three times. Just the blood, the letters, but I can feel her pointing the finger at me. All of them – pointing, horrified accusing faces. Like half of them wouldn't have done the same. Like half of them didn't. Maybe they're all getting dreams like this. That makes me feel a bit better. If it's not just me then it's doesn't sound so mental. If everyone is getting them maybe it really is a haunting and ghosts are a thing after all. I could go into school tomorrow and be like 'what's up with all these bloody letters stalking me when I'm trying to sleep?' And they'd all be like 'yeah, me too'. And we could have a laugh about it. I mean, I know she liked English but this is taking it to extremes, talk about obsessed. And the alphabet is for babies, right. Haha. Hahaha.

But maybe they didn't say something so awful. It's just me she's angry at.

I don't believe in ghosts, I really don't, so I don't know why I keep thinking that. She can't be angry. She's dead and she's gone and she can't be anything at all any more. Only losers believe in ghosts and jerks pretend to. I feel sick. YOU MAKE ME SICK. If it's not her then...

The blood is fading but I can still see the letters, dancing about the ceiling – white on little black squares. It isn't really the alphabet either, that was a lie, what I said. It's just some letters. The worst ones. Even if everyone else was getting dreams like this I wouldn't tell them what letters she's throwing at me. I watch them now, the three of them left over from the dream, still skitting about up there. Twat. STUPID COW. What do I want to watch them for? NUTTER. I shift my gaze about the room to try to shake them off but they follow. Y flitting over the curtain rail. O bouncing up and down on my wardrobe. U crawling down the wallpaper. Y O U twirling round the light cord. When they disappear inside the light shade, I actually breathe a sigh of relief. Until all the other letters come tumbling out the bottom.

D Y E O I S U T S T E O R D V E E

They're all jumbled up but I know what they say because they're my letters. I typed them. And they are coming for me now – raining, clattering, pounding down on me, burying me.

*   *   *

In the morning, Mum makes me go to school even though I look like death warmed up. I tell her that when she asks what's the matter with me now. I say I feel like death and I look like death warmed up and any good mother, any normal mother would notice. The least she can do is let me stay home. Everyone's parent's are supposed to be being *sensitive* with us *during this difficult time*.

She tells me not to be so hard-faced, how can I say things like that, how do I think she feels?

I don't know. I don't think I know how anyone feels. But I can't say that because she is looking at me, horrified, like no right person could behave like I am, so I just grab my bag and go. It doesn't matter if I've got the right books or not; the teachers are still letting us off with all sorts. It's the shock, Sir. We were all just too upset to concentrate on homework, Miss. Ever since Kelly... d.... People are so easy to manipulate when there's something they don't want to hear you say. It's so stupid. THICKO. I try not to think what Mum's face would look like if she could hear me, if she knew, if she ever found out.

     I'm just about to give the front door a really good slam when I remember my pillow. I thunder up the stairs again, dump my bag, and flip my pillow over to hide the mascara stains from where I cried last night. LOSER. There is no way in hell I'm having Mum find that. She'll only start asking questions and I don't need it from her right now. Shit. The other side is marked from the night before. SAD TWAT crying in your pillow like a BABY every night. Mum is on the stairs, wondering what I'm up to. I yank the duvet straight, tuck the bottom of it in, pull it up right over the stupid pillow. To really put her off investigating, I smooth the duvet as neat as I can and grab a pink stuffed dog that she won on the fair off the shelf and stick it at the top of the bed. There. What more can she ask?

I'm making my bed, I snap at Mum on my way past and she stares at me like she doesn't know me. I do slam the door.

*   *   *

I set out walking real slowly so I'll be late but I only get to the end of our road before the two brats from next door come tearing up behind me. They're all questions, looking for the gossip. Nasty little boys Stinking little first years, second years, whatever they are.. Like did I know her, she was in my year wasn't she, did I know, did I guess? Like is it true how she did it, and what they're saying, did we know? Do we know who did it? Do we know who said all that stuff?

     I tell them to piss off so loud that some little old lady on the other side stops dead and opens her mouth like a demented goldfish. I tell the brats to go to hell and stalk off as hard as I can. My legs are longer than theirs so they run to keep up but they haven't the breath for questions then so they drop off at the next corner. I storm on, poker legs, aches up my shins, scalded lungs, head down so no one will notice my face is boiling over with the effort of pretending that everything is normal. Escape is the next corner. I'm a mess, must look like, like some kind of... like her.

As if. I turn hard on my heel and almost fall off. Stupid shoes.
My hands are not shaking. No they're not. It's not funny. It's not funny. This is so not funny.
It's exactly the sort of thing I would laugh my head at if it wasn't me.
Pathetic.
PATHETIC.

*   *   *

I'm not late at all, I'm early because I can't slow down after that, in case the brats catch up. And everyone is talking about her. Still. It's been three days. Can we not move on to the X-Factor or Heat or bloody One Direction, or any other damn thing? The corridor goes quiet. Thirtyish faces swivel blank towards me. I disgust them. Well that's ok by me. Who cares?
Emily rushes off with her face in her hands. Two other saps go after her, giving me evils on the way. Gabby whispers that Em feels guilty for not doing anything. Everyone kicks at the scratches on the tiles. They all feel it. Except me. LOSER. Guilt is for losers. This whole school has gone to hell this last week. Nobody gave a shit about her before so I don't know why they're all pretending to care now. They all did it. They were all in it, nearly of them. It's not like we didn't mean it, just because she... yeah, is it?
Nobody will look at me.

*   *   *

I make it almost till break before I've had enough. They won't shut up about her. How sweet, how sad, how lonely, how awful. All through Biology and on into History. I curl my hands until my nails dig in and really start to hurt. Creeps. I want to jump up and thump the desk, point, yell at them that they all hated her, they all did it. They're all liars and two-faced bitches. And I hate her. I still hate her. I hate her right now.
I stop myself, just. I jam my hand up and ask to go to the toilet. Four maroon crescents score my palm but it's not like anyone's going to notice. Sir always lets girls go anyway but this week

he doesn't even roll his eyes.

*　　*　　*

I hate her. She's ruined everything. I hate her. She's ruined everything. I hate her.

I sit on the closed lid of the skanky toilet, past caring, kicking the door with every thought. There's a nice black rubbery smudge all up the bottom half of it. STUPID BITCH. Why did she have to go and do something so stupid? She always was a show off, putting her hand up in class, getting up on the stage in assembly, all that. She loved the attention. She did all that stuff so we'd look at her. Bit sad really. Totally SAD. Thought it would get her friends. MAD COW. We gave her attention didn't we? She got all the attention she could have wanted. I choke and realise I'm giggling. It's like in class when I'm trying to hold it in and there's something just too funny. My whole belly hurts. The giggles are rising out of me. I put my hands over my mouth again but I can't stop them.

If anyone hears me they'll think I've really gone NUTTER. I'd better get back to class before anyone does. God, I can't even have a quiet skive in the toilet without her ruining it. I bet she'd love all the attention she's getting now. I bet she is loving it. This is her gloating, I bet. I give the door one last really good kick. I hate her. Something cracks. It's a tiny satisfaction but it's the best thing that's happened all day.

The toilet door squeaks a new squeak as I stare in the mirrors opposite. I look like shit. No two ways. I should have put some make-up on or something, sorted my hair out, but I don't have the energy. The toilet door finally groans itself shut and that's when I see them. The letters.

YOU   directly over my head.
DES   VE   half hidden by the reflection of my face.

And the rest blocked by the rest of my body, just a T here, and E there. But I know what they say. Bright red. Someone must have painted them on while I was locked in there. They've even done them back to front so I can read them right in the mirror. How could they do that? They must have been dead quiet. How could they know? I want to scream. I feel it rising in my throat like the giggles did and it's almost out when I remember – this isn't real. I close my

eyes and try to ignore the letters that dance about in bright light now on the inside of my head.
  YOU DESERVE YOU DESERVE
  I hold myself still, still as I can. This isn't real. I can't stop shaking. I can't open my eyes in case they really are still there.
  The door swings open, the proper door to the corridor.
'What's up with you?' My eyes snap open. Two girls from 11S are looking at me like I'm some sort of freak. I push past them fast. FREAK.
  'Piss off.'
  I can hear them laughing all the way down the corridor.

* * *

I try to skive assembly. Can't take another expression of concern, or grief, or disbelief, or invitations to talk if there is anything... or any of that old bollocks. But I'm not going back in them toilets and there's no other really good places to hide. I'm hunched up on a windowsill round by the sixth form which is a pretty good spot for mitching off but I've no luck today – the bloody head of year comes past and catches me. I get hauled in late and made to sit at the back on my own. The whole year turns round to gawp. I hate the lot of them. And I still have to sit through all that sentimental crap. If anyone needs to talk. If anyone needs to get something off their chest. Do they get this stuff out of a book?
  And better to come forward. Hard to believe about our school, a school such as this. I hate this place. No stone left or something or other. It's like they're talking about catching whoever graffitied the Office door – which they never did. I switch off.
  Have to stay in all break though to get a bollocking and further expressions of concern. They're doing me a favour though really because who wants to hang out with the scum in my class anyway, not me.

* * *

Outside Maths, Gabby puts her arm around me and asks if I'm all right. SUCK UP. I swear at her really bad and she asks Miss if she can sit on the other side of the room with Chantelle. She's lucky I didn't punch her. LES. She wants some kind of heart-to-heart and the thought of that makes my skin crawl. She used to be my best friend in primary but now she's just so STUCK UP. I look over a couple of times, when I'm sure she's not looking at me. She looks a bit watery eyed. Chantelle is blocking her, putting her head close to Gabby's, passing her things, letting her copy her book so she doesn't have to look up at the board. What do I care?

Everyone is staring at me. Not when I look up. They all pretend to be working or talking, same as normal. But it's not normal. I can tell they're looking at me all the time whenever my head is down. I can feel it. It's like they think I'm some kind of time bomb, that I'm going to go off any second and do something dramatic like swear or burst into tears or run out.

* * *

I get chucked out of French for asking what the word for "suicide" is. It's just a word, Miss, keep your hair on, God. It's vocabulary isn't it? Topical.

I have to stand in the corridor for the rest of the lesson and I get detention for three days next week.

* * *

The afternoon is double IT but there is no way I am even going to touch a computer so I just walk out. What's the point?

* * *

I'm walking down our road when my phone trills. I haven't had any kind of message in days. Not since Kelly...

I stop to read it. A number I don't recognise. My thumb twitches over the screen.

ITS ALL YOUR FAULT

I laugh. Yeah right. Cos I was the only one. I didn't even start it.

I delete the message and I notice the time on my phone. 14.01. I can't go home. Mum finishes work at two so she'll be back in twenty minutes. She'll go mental at me if she catches me out of school again. I turn round and make for the park.

*   *   *

It's nice there when it's quiet, no screaming kids. I sit on a bench in the sun and close my eyes. I'm so tired. I could just sleep actually. That's a bit weird, sleeping on a park bench. TRAMP. But I'm not really sleeping, just resting a bit. My eyelids glow bright red from the inside and I can see those weird tiny veins, looking huge. I can't remember the last time I got a proper night's sleep. Before... How long ago was that? It's peaceful here, in the red glow, until the letters start to form.
        B   T   They dance about.
        C   I   Inside my eyes.
        H
My phone buzzes on the bench beside me. I jerk awake.
1 message.
Unknown number.
EVERYONE KNOWS WHAT YOU DID
    That's it, I'm going home. I need to go home. I need to be home right now. I grab my stuff and shove my phone in my pocket. My hands are so clumsy I miss the pocket and drop it. As it hits the ground it trills again. I snatch it up.
1 message.
I HATE YOU
I almost drop it again. I want to throw it down, stamp on it. I want to leave it there and walk away. But I love my phone. It was my birthday present. And Mum will kill me. Carefully, slowly, I slide it into my blazer pocket. I walk out of the park. If I just keep walking I can get home and go upstairs and shut myself in my room. I'll tell Mum I felt sick or something. I don't even care if she yells. If I can just get home it will all be ok. My phone knocks against my hip lightly with every step. I get all the way across the park and it doesn't go off. I start to breathe a bit more. I cross the road, head past the shops and still nothing. I can almost relax. It was nothing. Nothing to get worked up about. I must be really strung out if I'm letting a little thing that get to me. I try to laugh. Some primary school kids with their mums turn round and look at me like I've got horns sticking out of my head. I do laugh then. The mums tug the kids'

hands. Yeah, run away babies, I'm the big scary monster. I'm tough. I'm the bitch from hell, just ask my mates. Just ask Kelly. She'll tell you what I'm like.

I'm still laughing when my phone goes again.

* * *

And there it is. That message. My message. I'm not even surprised any more that it's come back to me.

And I'm standing in the middle of the pavement crying because it's true now. For the first time all those things I said are true, not for Kelly, but for me. I made that happen, that awful thing, I made her do it, and now she's made all those things true. The message on my screen is right. It's meant for me all right. All the letters fall into place.

* * *

YOU DESERVE TO DIE

Irish Roots
Gerry McCullough

Once inside the Hilton, he might have been anywhere in the world.

Outside, as they headed from the airport, everything had been different, new; leaving the darkness of the country roads, driving into streets where the headlights of the taxi glinted on the rain-bright trees that grew even in the heart of the city.

The driver said, in an accent weirdly like his granny's, 'You oughta get to see the countryside, son. Och, Belfast's great, but the country, the back of beyond, that's the real thing for youse Americans.'

Funny, in America he was 'Irish', but over here he was 'American'. Would there ever be a place where he could feel that he really belonged? Well, that was why he was here. To find it.

*   *   *

Next morning he rented a car, and drove to what his father, who had never been there, called 'our part of the world.' County Down. He'd heard of it all his life.

His grandfather Michael used to tell him that Michael's own father, Thomas Mulligan, had owned a farm in County Down, in the late nineteenth century.

As often happened in those days, Thomas married several times. Wife after wife died in childbirth, and Thomas ended up with twenty children. Farms were usually left to the eldest son, to keep the land together. But Thomas left each of his children part of the farm. The result was that none of them had enough land to support a family.

Mostly, they gave up the struggle, sold up, moved up to Belfast, or across the water to England. To a labouring or a factory job.

His grandfather Michael Mulligan travelled to America and did well there. By the time he died, he was a dollar millionaire. Liam remembered him well, a kind, dignified old man in his eighties, and his granny Molly, a bright, loving old lady who spoilt him with home baked soda bread and hugs and kisses.

History repeated itself. Michael left his money between his eight children, and after tax none of them had a particularly large amount to start life on.

Liam's father, Seamus Mulligan, became a lawyer. He was a shrewd man who put his money into the firm he worked for and ended up as a partner, and when his only son, Liam, graduated from High School, Seamus naturally hoped he would follow in his footsteps.

Liam didn't much want to be a lawyer. But he didn't want to be anything else in particular, either.

The idea of the farm back home in Ireland had begun to eat into him. Not that he wanted to be a farmer as such. But the idea was there in his head, swelling in size every day, until eventually, like a swiftly growing tumour, it ended by pushing everything else out.

To go over to Ireland. To find out what he could about his family's roots.

'Fair enough, Liam,' his father said. 'You're young yet. Take a year out. Go over and have a look round. But roots are strong, ugly things, son. Mostly, you can't feed on them. It's the apples that come from the tree that matter. Just as long as the roots are there, you've no need to be digging them up to look at them. Don't let yourself get dragged down trying. It's what you are yourself that matters. And after this one year, I want you to come back and train for a sensible life and a sensible job. Okay, not as a lawyer, if you don't want to.'

He said, 'Totally,' and his father gave him the money for his ticket, and a reasonable sum to keep him alive for the next year. Together with a worried look.

He landed in Belfast International Airport at eleven pm local time, early in June. He was fresh from graduation, travelling the world by himself for the first time. And he was in his homeland, the land his family came from. He was going to find his relations, to see the place where his great grandfather's farm had been.

There was so much to discover.

Setting out next morning in his rented car, he thought that it was right that the sun should be shining, casting its bright, cheerful light over everything, drying up the roads after last night's rain.

He turned off the motorway and there it was, County Down, the low rolling hills, green as the beer in New York pubs on St.

Patrick's Day, 'basket of eggs' formation. Little, bright-hedged country lanes, full of pale pink wild roses, sweet-smelling, creamy honeysuckle and hosts of white, lacy cow parsley; lanes leading from one tiny village to another, more and more confusing the further south he went. He followed a signpost for 'Ballymore: 2 miles' then came out at a crossroads where the sign told him that to reach Ballymore, he should drive 1 mile back. He didn't particularly want to get to Ballymore, but he couldn't understand how he'd missed it. Unless it was the two or three bungalows he'd passed along the road?

It amused him.

But presently, he wasn't laughing. He needed to find the right place. Ardmore. His grandfather Michael's birthplace. Not far from Ballymore on the map.

Eventually, driving back and forwards, covering far too many miles, he found it.

It wasn't much bigger than the other tiny places he'd passed through that day. A few small cottages, a church, a shop, two pubs. A small Housing Executive Estate along the road a bit, and a very upmarket restaurant, The Old Hayloft, a converted barn, with plenty of parking space. He pulled in, and went into the bar.

Seated at the counter with a pint of Guinness (he had been brought up right, to drink the black stuff), he took a satisfying sip, and looked round. An elderly man smoking a dirty old pipe gave him a friendly smile.

'Slainte!' Liam said, raising his glass, just as his father had always done.

A youngish man in a shabby denim jacket scowled at him and muttered something Liam didn't catch. He stood up and brushed rudely past him, almost spilling Liam's pint on the way out.

'What was that for?' Liam wondered aloud.

'Och, pay no attention to Billy O'Neill!' the old man told him, shrugging. 'He's a right bigot. Now me, I live and let live. Cheers, son!' He raised his own glass to Liam.

Liam didn't understand. But he didn't like to ask more about the incident. Anyway, he had more important things to find out.

'Are there any Mulligans living around here?' he asked the old man. 'That's my family name. I'd like to meet up with some of them if possible.'

'No shortage!' the old man chuckled. 'Martha Mulligan lives

just down the road, I'll point out her cottage to you. And she'll put you in touch with the rest of the clatter of them.'

The woman behind the bar pushed her dark hair back from her thin face and sniffed. 'Don't know why you'd be sending the poor wee lad to see thon auld slut!' she said. 'A disgrace, so she is. Shaming us all!'

'Och, Annie, catch yerself on!' said the old man. 'The lad wants to meet his relations. Martha's all right. Live and let live, I say.' He seemed proud of his attitude, happy to repeat the same words any number of times, expecting praise for what he said.

He hobbled to the door with Liam to put him in the right direction. The house – it wasn't what Liam would have called a cottage, two stories and no sign of a thatch – was only a step away.

Liam was nervous. He didn't want to get off on the wrong foot.

He knocked on the door, and presently a dog began barking, and he could hear a voice loudly shushing it, and then the door opened on the chain.

'Yes?'

She wasn't that old, maybe eight or so years older than him, say around twenty-six, but there was something cautious about her that seemed older.

'Martha Mulligan?'

'That'll be me Granny.'

'I wondered if I could come in and talk to you. I'm your long lost cousin from America.' He grinned nervously, and the girl's pale, fine-boned face broke into a friendly, encouraging smile.

'Come in.' She stood back from the door, pushed it shut to release the chain, then opened it again.

'There's been a lot of break-ins in these parts, you mightn't think it, we have to be careful.'

It might have been New York.

'Me Granny's in here.' She opened a door on the right of the tiny hall. 'She's been poorly, she might not feel able to talk for long.'

As he followed her into the small dark living room, a voice mumbled something from the corner.

'Who's this gawky looking bit of string, Katy? Yer new boy?'

He knew he was too thin for his height and not too good at holding himself up straight. But he hated her for saying it. He felt his face grow red and angry.

'Granny, this here's our cousin from America, what did you say your name is?'

'Liam Mulligan.'

Martha Mulligan was sitting in an elderly rocking chair, a rug over her knees, nursing a half-empty cup of tea. She was quite old, he thought. At least sixty. Maybe nearly seventy. She peered at him, finally spoke.

'Liam? What sort of a name's that, son?'

'Well – Irish?'

'You're in Ulster here, son!'

He didn't understand.

'My great grandfather came from this village,' he said, deciding to get right down to it. 'Thomas Mulligan.'

'Thon auld git?' She spluttered into her tea, dribbling it down her chin. 'Who'd want to know about him?'

'You remember him?' he asked eagerly.

'Remember him? I'll never forget him, the auld devil.'

'Why, what – ?'

'Did nothing but drink himself silly from morn till night, and not a penny left to feed the family, so my da used to say. Not that I'd believe much from him, mind you!'

'Your father was one of Thomas's sons?' He was getting excited. 'Did you know my own Grandfather – Michael Mulligan?'

'That skitter! Turned his coat and took off to America with his new Fenian wife, and left me to bring up his weans on nothing. Listen, he was my da, d'ye think I wouldn't remember him?'

She must be his auntie, then. But his grandfather's children were all born in America. Had he been married before?

'I don't follow you?' he said.

'Why should you?' She made a noise between a snarl and a laugh. ' It's not a story you'd expect to hear. So you want to know all about your family background, do you? I'll tell you, then – '

'Now, Granny,' Katy interrupted anxiously, 'don't be getting yourself all worked up with that ancient history!'

'The boy wants to know about his family! Hasn't he got a right to know if he wants to? Come over here, you, boy.' She beckoned him closer, twisting about in the rocking chair, leaning forward to get nearer to him. Liam came towards her. Her body smell was stronger close to, and her yellow teeth gleamed in an unpleasant smile. 'Away you and put the tea on, Katy.'

'Don't believe a word she says, now,' Katy whispered to him as she went. He suddenly noticed how pretty she was. 'She's a desperate old liar.'

Martha Mulligan began to talk. She talked and talked. How hard her life had been. Her drunken boyfriend who beat her up every Saturday night. Her struggles to bring up the children.

He wasn't interested. This wasn't what he wanted to hear. He wanted to know about his great grandfather, about the farm. He wanted to know where it had been. And about his own grandfather.

It came suddenly, in the middle of her ramblings.

'Me da was never the same after me ma died so young. They had three children. I was the oldest. He was a man who couldn't be without a woman. He used to go out to the pub and pick up some slut, and bring her home. But once I got to be fourteen, he didn't see the need any more to go out of the house. And, there, I didn't know any different.'

He wasn't sure he had understood her properly. He must have got it wrong.

'What do you mean?' he stammered.

'What do you think?' Martha Mulligan leered at him.

He didn't want to understand. She couldn't mean –

Then he realised, with a stab of relief, that she was probably off her head. Making it up, like Katy said.

Or, even, talking about some other family of Mulligans. There must be plenty of them in this country, for goodness sake.

The old woman suddenly turned round and reached over the back of her chair to a low table, half hidden from him up until now by Martha herself and by the rocker. When she turned round to him again, there was something in her hand. A photograph in a scratched frame. She thrust it out at him.

'Here! Take hold of thon!'

He took it, although something in him didn't want to.

'That's me when I was a wean. And that's my da.'

A pretty, fair-haired child, about eight or nine, looked out at him from the photo with laughing eyes. She was holding the hand of a good-looking young man, not more than thirty. It was undoubtedly his grandfather, Michael. So much younger. But unmistakeable.

And the child? Could it be the ancient crone dribbling malevolently at him from the rocking chair?

He tried to trace the features of the fair-haired child of the photo in the wizened old face in front of him, and with a feeling of horror realised that it was the same face. Ruined by time and grief and bitterness, but the same.

A picture sprang up in his mind of his grandfather Michael as he had known him, and with the picture came pain.

He had almost ceased to listen, when Katy's entrance with the tea called him back to the present. He stood up to take the tray from her, and to set it down on the big table by the window.

Katy poured out the tea and offered him a plate of shop bought biscuits.

'What've you been saying, Granny?' she asked the old woman anxiously. 'You shouldn't go over all that old stuff any more. Let it go. Here's someone from America, come to be friendly. Be nice to him, Granny, for dear sakes.'

But Martha Mulligan paid no heed. She seized the fresh cup of tea Katy handed her, and went on talking, an angry note in her voice.

'Why should I let it go? It's my life I'm talking about here, Katy! My life! If he's from America, he's the first for fifty or more years! Yes,' she went on, mumbling half to herself, so that Liam had to strain to hear what she was saying. He knew he was missing many of the words, and thought he was a fool to try so hard to hear them. 'It was all right at first. I loved him, more fool me! I was happy, didn't know no better. Then he met up with this Fenian girl from across the valley, and started going with her. I was seven months gone with Katy's da by that time. I was angry – jealous. One night he brought her back home with him.' She stopped for a moment to drink some of her tea. 'This here's too hot, Katy! Give us a taste more milk in it for dear sakes!' When Katy supplied the tea with milk to Martha's satisfaction, she sipped again, and said grudgingly, 'Ah! That's more like it, girl.' Then she turned her attention back to Liam. 'Where was I? The night he brought the wee bitch home with him? Oh, aye. It came to a knockdown fight between her and me. I won! Oh, I won, all right!' She grinned savagely. 'I chased her out of the house with my da's big hammer. Didn't hit her. Might have, I was that angry.' Liam saw with repulsion that something – a tear? – was dripping from the end of her bony nose. Martha paused again to give it a cursory wipe on the corner of her cardigan. 'It wasn't any good,' she said. 'He went out of the house after her like he was on fire and jumping for the water! Never came back near any of us. Not even when his own wee son was born. Went to America. Left me to bring them all up myself.

'An evil old git, I think now. I was a right fool to myself, letting him away with all he did. But there, I wasn't old enough to know better...' Her voice tailed away.

He looked at her as more tears started to trickle down her withered face. He was shaking. He didn't know how much to believe. Could this be his kind, dignified Grandfather she was talking about? It was all so disgusting. He backed away from her.

Katy followed him out into the kitchen.

'I'll have to go, now,' he said. 'Thanks for the tea.'

'Don't think too badly of my granny,' Katy said as he tried to get past her and out into the fresh air. Her face was anxious, full of something that he thought, later, might have been love. 'Have a bit of pity on her, won't you? She's difficult to take, but she's had a hard life, see? People thought badly of her, called her names, left her to get on by herself. But none of what happened was her fault, was it? She was only a wean. Don't – '

Liam didn't want to know. He pushed past her, almost ran down the path, without a goodbye, closing his ears to whatever else she might say, and reached the car.

It was difficult to get it started. Partly the unaccustomed gear stick. Partly the tears blinding his eyes.

He found his way back to the main road. After a few miles, he pulled in, and dived out just in time to throw up on the grass verge. He wiped his mouth with a tissue as he got back into the car and tried to recover.

What had he just heard? Did he have to believe it? Things like that only happened in books and films, didn't they? *Chinatown*, that sort of thing? Not in his own family!

'Roots can be ugly. Don't let them drag you down,' his father had said. How much did his father know? If he knew about this stuff, why hadn't he warned Liam?

He had wanted to know about his own roots. He'd thought it would help him to know who he was. But this wasn't who he was! This was nothing to do with him! There must be more to find out –

but he knew he didn't want to. All he wanted to do with these roots he'd dug up was to get rid of them for ever. Burn them, trample on them, pound them into ashes.

      Liam went home the next day, on the first flight he could get. Back to America. Back to his father.

Years later, adolescence behind him, he came to see the place again.
      Martha was dead by then. And Katy didn't want to know him.

The Man Code
Conor Mc Varnock

He'd never considered himself to be the sort of guy to have a moral code, but *you know that there are rules though, don't you?* You have to have something to tell your kids, *that's something you're supposed to do isn't it?* Stevie Copeland had been having these sorts of thoughts a lot since his girl had got pregnant. The news really had changed everything, even though he hadn't decided what he was going to do about it. He was going to be somebody's Dad whatever he did. A lot of new thoughts had been coming into his head that he wouldn't have even considered a year ago, not all of them good. This one had been surfacing a lot lately, about the rules, the sort of thing you'd want your son to know if you want him to grow up to be one of the good ones. A good lad like his Da. Or on the off chance it was a girl, you'd want her to know what a real man was supposed to be so when the time came she'd be able to pick herself a good one.

What was it? A line from a film or something; *Never complain, never explain.* Too fuckin' right. Some shit is going to happen, no point throwing a wobbler every time something doesn't go quite your way. Explain? Too much of that and you sound like you're just making excuses for yourself. Good one, top of the list.

Being a man was more than just being a tough guy. He knew some hard nuts and he knew them well enough that he understood that with the real hard lads it was just in their nature, you either had it or you didn't. A real man didn't just go around starting fights with randomers either, or get in anybody's face over nothing, but if somebody crosses you, always get your own back.

And girls? Je-sus there should be a whole book of rules devoted just to them. But off the top of his head the important stuff was, don't cheat if you've a Woman you even half-way care about unless you know she's done the dirty on you, don't mix your love life up with your work and don't mess with the crazy ones.

Bro's before hoes, it's a bit obvious and a bit American but it was true. Women would come and go but your mates were the people you're supposed to have around you your whole life. And you especially don't ever let a fuck get in the way of a friendship, you never went after a girl your mate was looking into, even if you knew for sure he wasn't in with a shot. It's a bit of a shit one when somebody does it to you so don't be that guy and do it to anybody else.

It's a big bad world out there and if he expected his kid to be fully innocent of it he would be putting him at a terrible disadvantage. God knows he was no angel himself. *But if you are going to be dodgy* he reasoned *you don't mess or scam with anybody who is actually an innocent, anybody who doesn't have it coming and you never rip off a mate.* He'd been stroked, sold overpriced drugs and dud pills by people who knew rightly that they were garbage and it really wasn't cool. No way was any kid of his going to pull that sort of crap, not if he could help it.

This was just some of the various bits and pieces that were in his head as he made the drive up the Shore Road to see Tall Paul. *No point dwelling on it though,* he thought as he approached the left turn off the road, today he was a man with a plan and that plan was a fairly important one with implications that could reverberate into the rest of his life. Part A of the plan involved going to see Paul at his gaff in White Abbey.

Paul lived in one of the streets off Station Road. Stevie parked his car in the grounds of the hospital then took a circuitous route through several back alleys and across wasteland until he was at the side entrance to Paul's house. This was exactly the route that Paul insisted his business contacts make when approaching his house for anything related to work. It all seemed a bit unnecessary, when you dealt in illegal substances for a living you could never be too careful but Paul seemed to be cautious to the point of paranoia. This once however Stevie appreciated the lengths Paul had insisted he go to to cover his tracks, even if he half suspected that he was pure doing it to annoy him.

He texted Tall Paul when he got out of the car so he was a bit hacked off that when he got to the back of Paul's house the gate hadn't been left open for him, it wasn't locked but the way the thing was set up it was always a melt trying to jimmy the thing open. It took about two minutes of concerted effort, which felt like a very long time. Stevie took this imagined slight and subconsciously stored it away with the list of petty justifications he would use later should the need arise. Entering the kitchen by the back door he rapped the counter to announce his arrival.

"Come on in," he heard Paul shout from the living room.

He walked in to find that Paul was sitting on the sofa smoking a joint with some subtitled film on the TV, a copy of some book with a very serious looking black and white photo on the front lying spread open face down on the coffee table. This was how it always was when you came to see Paul in his own house, him sitting with his feet up smoking a J and doing something pretentious and conspicuously not playing the X-Box like anybody normal. Stevie had a sneaking suspicion that the routine of texting before hand and taking a round-about way to the house had less to do with security and more to do with giving Paul the necessary time to construct these little scenes to make himself look clever. Not that he wasn't bright or anything, he was one of those guys that always seem to know about what's going on and with that shaven baldy dome, pointy beard and glasses he looked like a proper egg-head, but soon he would see how smart he really is.

"Alright mucker, how's the form?" asked Paul, passing him over the joint, which Stevie declined.

"Not bad mate," Stevie replied and then he sat down and they did the obligatory five to ten minute conversation you did when you went to somebody else's house to buy drugs. Paul asked after Charlene and the pregnancy and even jokingly inquired as to when he was thinking of making an honest woman of her. Stevie asked after Paul's cousins who he knew causally and his latest attempts to acquire funding for his PHD. He'd known Paul about six years on and off. They were both about the same age and Paul was only a few years ahead of him on the clubbing scene in Belfast when he started going to nights himself. When he first met him he'd been in much the same position that he found himself in now, someone who wasn't a "Drug Dealer" as such, just someone who happened to do drugs themselves and supplemented some of their partying by selling a bit on here and there, mostly to their mates. Somewhere along the way though, Paul had brought his game up to the next level. He'd got a connection to somebody who was importing and wholesaling the stuff as well as the necessary line of credit and social capital to function as a full time dealer. Over the years he'd partied with him loads of time and they'd had some mad wiped-out conversations at after-parties, some of them in this very room.

Eventually the conversation wound its way round to the

inevitable matter of business. The deal was the same as had been done between the two of them many times before. Paul produced a plastic bag filled with white powder the size of a baby's head from a metal strong-box wedged between the sofa and the wall and passed it to Stevie.

"There you go mate, two solid ounces of your bog standard shitty Belfast coke", he said with a self deprecating smile. "There's some plastic Tupperware containers in the kitchen and some scales on top of the microwave if you want to weigh it."

He considered it for a second then thought better of it. He'd never measured the product on buying it before and he didn't want to do anything unusual that would raise suspicions now. Besides, when he'd bought ounces of cocaine from Paul before the weight had always been bang on, or even a little bit over, and anyway, whatever he sold the Coke for would be pure profit.

"Nah you're all right mate."

"Any trouble getting it sold, you give me a shout. I reckon I know a few guys looking some for next weekend."

"Should be grand like, I already have somebody lined up for at least half an ounce and a couple of my regulars ringing me about this weekend already."

"No worries then big lad. Safe home and tell the Missus I was askin' after her."

And with that he was away. He felt a bit giddy in the run back to the car and there, motoring down the shore road back into Belfast it hit him: a visceral sinking sensation, like a hand clamped to the pit of his stomach, pulling downwards. This was really happening. Like all good plans it was simple enough. Get coke from Paul on tic to sell on then get money from buyer on the promise of the coke to come later. Stroke the pair of them, pocket the money and product and disappear before either of them start looking for their end of the deal. Between the money he would be getting tonight and whatever he could sell these ounces of coke for over in England he'd have about four grand when all was said and done. Enough to start a new life with and give his new family a bit of a chance. Even if it didn't work out with Charlene he would at least have a wee nest egg of cash to leave to her and he could do a phantom with a relatively clean conscience.

As he sat in the upstairs of The Front Page awaiting the buyer he congratulated himself on how nervous he wasn't. *Surely there has to be more to it than this?* The ease with which he had deceived Paul had him flushed with the feeling of his own smartness. He felt like an adult for the first time in his 26 years. This was the sort of shit you saw guys pulling in films or on TV. To be fair, those guys usually came a cropper but this was real life and that wouldn't happen to him. He was so clever he had fooled Tall Paul, who was no dozer himself, and any minute now would come along another wee chicken, ripe to be plucked.

This chickens' name was Crystal. *Odd name for a girl* he always thought, *love to know where it came from*. He pondered this while he was waiting for her. Was her Ma some hippy that was into all that crystal shit? Some rich bitch with a whole collection of crystal necklaces or some aul alcho' that loved the sparkly wine? Some combination of the above? All three? There was nothing about the wee girl that really gave any of that away. She dressed a bit Hippy, but the make up and tatts were pure rock chick. Her accent was definitely Northern Irish but it was a bit hard to place from where exactly. She talked some shite and used some big words like she'd been to Uni, but there was something very un-studenty about her too, a bit too innocent with it to be at all clever. Still, there were plenty of thick students. He'd asked after her in the run up to tonight around some of their mutual friends, not in an obvious way but so as to make out like he was interested in her. Not that he cared much about her, but he didn't want to be messing with anyone with family connections to the paramilitaries. Nothing like that as far as he could tell, a suggestion of her coming from money but nothing definite.

It shouldn't matter anyway, by this time next week he should be in Durham. Charlene had the connections over that way, nobody knew him there and nobody who knew him here could have any notion he'd ever be near the place. He might as well be on the fucking moon for all the chance of Tall Pauls' Provie mates or anybody else from Belfast finding him.

One thing about her. She seemed a bit mental or something. Not that he was an expert or anything but there was something about her that was a bit odd, more than being just a bit "kooky". He remembered having that feeling that first time he met her a few months ago. Jonty had introduced them.

Jonty was his mate, and had been for some time but he was a

wee bit out of his circle these days, had a proper job and didn't get off his face except maybe like once or twice every couple of months, not like the old days back in school. He hadn't seen Jonty in a while, then from out of nowhere he gets a phone call to meet in the back-bar at Lavery's and shows up with this girl in tow. He didn't say anything but he was obviously bustin' to get into her, and meeting him here to buy a gram of cocaine was obviously part of it, basking in his own reflected glory like "look at me, look at how dangerous I am, I l know guys I can get coke off, I'm practically Al Pa-fawkin'-chino, go on love gis a buck at ye", acting all cool and familiar around the drugs and talking all West-Belfast like he used to before he went away to university. Not that Stevie minded or anything, he was a mate after all, or that it seemed to be doing the lad any good. All Jontys' efforts to seem like anything more than the nice-wee-hard-working-good-9-5-job middle class boy that he was bounced clean off her.

Actually, the way she seemed to practically ignore Jonty after they'd got their gram of white, when she wasn't making disparaging jokes about him were the first sign that she was a bit odd. The way she didn't get anyone else's jokes then pretend to get them when they were explained even though she still blatantly didn't understand them, the way she skweed like a little girl at some other birds Pokémon back pack, the weird rambling conversation about some person she didn't even know herself and nobody was actually interested in. It all added up to make him think she was on something already unless this was how she actually got on all the time. The couple of times he'd met her since (one more drug deal through Jonny, two random bumping-intos in town and the conversation in the smoking area outside the Duke of York that had led to tonight) had convinced him that yes, this was just how she was. Mental.

And here she was, lolloping around the corner and shooting him a single jazz-hand wave and open mouthed shake of a head to say hello. She bounced up onto the raised seating area between the bar and the stage area and swung in beside him to give him a weird elbow-y hug.

"Hi-i!" she said. Then she leaned in and whispered in his ear "you got the stuff?"

"Not on me." He said back quietly. "I told you, I can't be carrying around an ounce of white, give me the money now I'll get you it tomorrow night."

"Pinkie promise?" she said sticking her little finger out to him, her tongue absent mindedly playing with her lip piercing.

"Sure, you have the money ready?" he said, snaking his middle finger around hers then retracting it.

"That's not how you do it," she pouted.

Right that second, the man didn't give a fuck how you did it. The celebratory bump of cocaine he had sniffed out of the crevice between his thumb and forefinger in the bar's toilets had given him a nervous excitement and he could have happily throttled her for dicking around like this. However causing a scene wouldn't get him what he wanted and his better judgement took over. He smiled and made an elaborate show of mimicking her hand gesture exactly.

This pleased her. She hunched her shoulders and pressed her fists into her chin and let out a small giggle, then straightened her posture and in a suddenly mature tone said, "but yah, I have it." She looked around the bar to ensure no one was giving them any undue attention and took a thick wad of notes out of the pocket of her Jeans, and slipped it and her hand into his pocket. Then she leaned over with her hand still in his pocket and whispered, "with a big wad like that in your trousers the least you could do is buy a girl a drink", then broke the moment by giggling like an adolescent girl at the hilarity of her own joke.

"Seriously though", she said, again apparently sincere, "you go to the bar, I just got here and I'm dying for a Magners'".

Stevie wanted to be away, and yet with the business concluded he felt an immense weight had lifted from him, an elation like he'd had on leaving Paul's house, but more so. Most of the work was done, all he had to do now was get on the bus from the Europa to the ferry, nobody would expect him to leave the city that way and getting the coke past the security there was a piece of piss. Then get the bus over to the mainland, off at Glasgow, take the trains that would get him to Durham and that would be it. Once there put all the coke into gram bags and a couple of weekends in Newcastle and he would be shot off as much of it as he wanted to sell, obviously he'd keep a bit for himself, and he'd have more money than he would know what to do with. Sure, he could stand to buy Crystal a drink and himself another pint, he could even sit and sip over it, let Crystal waffle whatever inane shite came into her head at him and take his time just listening to the banging Dub-Step mix the guy on the decks was kicking out. He gave Crystal a tenner out of his wallet to go to the bar and get the round in, and that was just what happened. Just sitting there feeling that rush of power from the ground into the soles of his feet, to his kneecapps, to his balls, to the top of his head and beyond, and Crystal and the deep, crunchy music.

Then, the atmosphere in the room lifted as a new DJ took over on the decks, dropping a slow song with a simple clear line of piano over the pervious harsh cacophony of breaks and beats that had occupied the aural space just seconds before. As the soft sweet female vocals kicked in Crystals' face lit up with recognition.

You say you'll be there fo-or me
In times-of-trouble when-I-need-you when I'm dow-own.

"Oh my god I love this I can't believe they're playing it!"

And likewise you need friendship,
and from my side its-been-love but I see lately things-have-been-changing

"Oh. My. God! We are so dancing to this."

You've got goals to achieve, but the-roads-you-walk are broad-and-heartless,

"I'm dancing to this one, and you are too, mister!"

You throw stones!

"Aww, C'mon!"

Can't-you-see that I-am-human, I-am-bleeding

"Alright then."

But you don't give a damn……..

She stood up and took Stevie's hand and led him down the

steps and onto the designated dancing zone at the front of the stage. Normally he would have resisted but he thought, yeah sure, I can dance, I'm pulling off the stroke of the century, I am Batman, I can do anything. It was a pleasant enough tune anyway, he'd danced to worse.

Then the tune started changing, as they danced a little to limber themselves, the beat kicked in and started building the tune up towards something. Crystal swayed gently in time to the bass, arms held out at an odd angle, eyes half closed, totally at one with the music.

Then at almost exactly one minute into the song something strange happened, after the build up reached a crescendo, rich electric guitar cords crashed down on top of the tune like the breaking and crashing of a wave coming in off the ocean. Crystal rocked her body, grinding from the pelvis up perfectly matching the ups and downs of the riff. At that point Stevie started noticing things. Things like the curve of her breasts, the smoothness of her belly and that ass she had on her. Her eyes were wide open now and looking straight at Stevie. They said "I see you. I see you seeing me and I see you seeing me seeing you." Her lips were parted in a smile.

It was on.

Stevie continued to dance to the rest of the song in a mindless daze, not registering his own movements, all consciousness intensely focused on her. The song ended and she gave him another hug, this one less elbow-y and more intimate and followed up with a light kiss to the side of his face. It wasn't long after they had sat down that someone suggested they go somewhere more private to celebrate the conclusion of their transaction with a couple of lines from Stevie's personal stash. This, he thought, was going to be the culmination of a very profitable weekend. One last fuck with something young and hot before the drudge of domesticity he was about to subject himself to. One last good piece to say goodbye to his native city. The fact that he was about to rob this girl of a small but substantial sum of money did not enter into these thoughts, but had he cared to examine them in relation to each other he would have found that they didn't detract from each other, but rather made the whole thing that little bit sweeter.

She kissed him the first time just before they left the club. The taxi ride was hot, heavy and apparently instantaneous, time and space between the bar and the sofa in Stevie's flat confounded the laws of physics, melting entirely out of existence out of memory and into one long wet embrace. On the sofa in the front room they were, as they had been, all hands and teeth and tongues.

It was Crystal who finally broke the embrace off.

"I need to go to the little girls' room, I'll just be a second, could you do us a couple of lines while I freshen up?"

She got up and he took the gram bag he had on him and put it on first DVD case to hand.

"Oh yeah I nearly forgot I had these."

She took out her purse and took a small blue pill out of it, then she put it on the end of her tongue and leaned over to him, French-kissed it into his mouth giving him a good look down her cleavage.

"Back in a mo'."

He put the empty *Saw II* case on his knee and tap-tapped a small pile of cocaine out of the bag. He began the process of arranging the coke into lines. Stevie had spent a lot of time over the last couple of years arranging small piles of white powder like this into lines, and he could probably do it in the dark just on pure muscle memory, but after a couple of minutes of chopping, for some reason he just couldn't get his hands to work. His fingers couldn't hold the credit card with their usual dexterity and his hands felt somehow too big to do what they were meant to. The third time he dropped the card onto the lines he gave it up.

Jesus, I don't remember having that much to drink.

He tried to set the DVD case back on the table but by now his limbs had developed a slack bendy feeling he usually associated with ket. He set it down half on-half off the table and it gently tipped and fell off, spilling half the white powder onto the floor. Everything he did with his body seemed to be happening a long way away. Panic gripped him and he went to stand up but he seemed to have a large invisible lead weight resting softly on his lap like a sleeping spaniel. Unable to stand, he tried to sit upright but the leaden feeling had reached his head and the top of his chest.

He saw Crystal coming back into the room and tried to tell her not to take any of those pills but he only managed to burble incoherently in her general direction. Not that it would have mattered, she was on the phone, engrossed in conversation.

"Yeah it worked a treat! The dirty bastard couldn't keep his hands off me."

Something was amiss.

"Don't be like that, it got us inside the flat didn't it?"

'Something' flared into being within him. In a less confused state he would have recognised it as rage.

"Yeah, out for the count by the looks of it."

He could just about recognise that the last statement referred to him and more of the 'something' surged in him, lining his stomach with cold liquid silver, as he heard his address being given over the phone. But it didn't really seem to matter, it was all going on somewhere far away and he was falling back

down

    a

        long dark shaft

            into

                somewhere

else..

         *   *   *

When he came round in the harsh light of the early hours, the first thing he did was puke. He was stiff and his movements were jerky but he could stand. His body felt sore and his right eye wouldn't open. He assumed that this was the after-effects of whatever had happened to him until he saw himself, scowling with incomprehension into the mirror in the hallway. His eye was swollen and caked with dried blood. Somebody had hit him. Not just hit him, kicked the shit out of him. He pulled up his shirt to reveal big purple welts and he didn't even have to look at his balls because he knew that feeling from before, even though nobody had kicked him there since school you just never forget that feeling.

Discrete pieces of information started to connect with each

other as some of the events of the last night began to return. Crystal had gave him something to knock him out when he thought he was getting, what? Ecstasy, Viagra or something. Not a fucking roofie or whatever it was. Some guy had come over and did this to him. Some FUCKING FUCKER! *Who though? Jonty?* He dismissed that idea as soon as he had it, Jonty wouldn't do that to him and was too much of a BITCH PUSSY FAGGOT to do something like this (though he still had that kernel of resentment in him against Jonty for just putting the wee hooir in his orbit and physical vengeance would be extracted at some point in the future).

If Crystal was smart, and he was beginning to think that she was probably a bit smarter than she was letting on, just like all women, then her partner in crime would be somebody he didn't know or could never have met.

He would never know who did this to him.

He raged and kicked the sofa hard, putting a hole in the faux-leather and stubbing his toe on the metal frame underneath. The room was in an even bigger mess than he remembered it and he looked around it knowing he had been robbed. His wallet was empty, they'd taken all the money he had and the cards and even the spare condom he had in the hidden compartment behind the card slots. The spilled coke was missing but there were traces of lines on the glass surface of the table next to the bag, now empty. He could smell the unmistakable smell of sex in the room too.

That thought of what Crystal and her mystery man had been doing when he was unconscious *in his own fucking living room* sent him over the edge and he howled in rage again. Rage turned quickly to panic; *isn't there something really important I'm supposed to do today?*

He ran upstairs, his bedroom was a mess, the contents of the shelves had been rid out and turfed onto the floor, his mattress was still on the bed but it was upside down. The strong box in which he kept was on top of it, open face down. Everything in it of any value, his cash savings, his Granda's decommissioned WW2 Pistol, all his gear, including the two-ounce bag of cocaine that he had pinned his future hopes and dreams on: gone.

The implications of this hit him all at once and he sat down and put his head it his hands. The basic unfairness of it hit him in waves; *so close to getting there, that sneaky bitch, why does this have to happen to me?* Already in the back of his mind he was making his own excuses to himself, reconstructing and distorting his memory of events to make him the complete victim and rehearsing the spiel he would give to other people. Convincing Charlene to pack in her job and have the baby over in Britain had been enough of a head-melt, it was only the prospect of the money that was coming their way that had tipped the scales. It was going to take a lot of talking to her for her not to chuck him. He'd run right up into his overdraft over the last couple of weeks on the expectation of having the money later, without the coke or the money from Crystal he was flat broke. If he went on his hands and knees to her she'd take him in, skint as he was, but it would always hang over them. He knew he would literally never hear the end of it, and now he would be tied to her and the baby forever. The long sleepless nights, shitty nappies and shittier jobs, the responsibilities and his money never quite being his own again loomed at him out of an endless grim future.

The salt from the tears pooling it his eyes stung the cuts on his face as he picked up the house phone from the night stand and began to dial Charlene's number.

Garantan
H.D. Ferres

All characters in this story are entirely fictitious as is the estate.

Tuesday
Peter looked across the table as the committee finally reached the last item on the agenda, 'Any Other Business.' He glanced at his silent mobile phone as he held it under the table. Five missed calls from the same unknown number.
"Excuse me, Chairman, Committee Members, apologies, something has come up," Peter said. A couple of the members glared at him as he rose to leave.

* * *

Closing the door quietly, Peter listened to his voicemail.
"Lord Sexton, Chief Superintendent Daniel O'Riordan, County Mayo Garda Siochana here, Please phone me on 0353 949038211 as a matter of urgency."
He hurried out of the building. The Palace of Westminster was the last place he wanted to make this call. In the relative privacy of the lawn, he dialed the number.
"Lord Sexton, unfortunately I have to inform you that your employee Sean Cooney was found with a fatal bullet wound to the head at eleven am this morning. He was driving your vehicle, Grey Ford Mondeo, registration number 99-C-34961, which swerved and hit the main gates to your estate."
"Sean. Why? Oh my God. I asked him to take the car for its MOT. I had to be at a meeting.......Yes Superintendent; I'll get the first possible flight across and inform you of my eta. Thank you." Peter felt sick. He staggered out through the pedestrian gate.
"Are you alright Sir?" asked the Policeman on guard duty.
"Oh yes thanks, just got some bad news," Peter replied.

* * *

In the quietest corner of St Stephens Tavern, hand shaking, he swallowed a mouthful brandy. That bullet was for me, he shuddered. He hadn't told his wife about the death threats. Sean warned him. He'd heard them in the village. He'd trusted Sean. It was the first and last time Sean had driven the Ford. Damned meetings, he thought. He picked up his mobile phone:

"Hello Darling," he said.

"Peter, when are you coming home? The boys are being impossible. Christopher's just taken off on the quad bike," Daphne said.

"I'm so sorry I can't help you with that Darling, I have to rush back to Ireland," Peter said.

"What; again? I need you here. You sound a bit odd. Is everything OK?" Daphne asked.

"Sean Cooney's been shot dead. He was driving my car."

"What? Who's Sean Cooney? Why was he driving your car? "Daphne asked.

"Daphne, I told you, Sean Cooney was my caretaker and manager. He was taking the car for its MOT because I asked him to," Peter replied.

"Oh Peter how awful. Why was he shot? Did they think it was you?" Daphne asked.

"Look, I just don't know, and I'm not jumping to any conclusions. The Irish Police want to interview me so I'll be on the next flight I can get," Peter replied.

"Oh I wish you'd never taken on that God forsaken place. I'm so worried about you," Daphne said.

"I'll keep you posted," Peter said.

Wednesday

Travelling on the Gatwick Express Peter thought about his wife and sons. Christopher and Giles like coming over to Garantan with me. They like the wild landscape of the West of Ireland as much as I do. It's such a contrast to Wiltshire. Daphne's one visit was enough for her. I wish she didn't distrust the Irish so much.

Peter let the Irish Times slip out of his hands and rustle to the floor as the Air Lingus pilot announced that they were due to land at Knock Airport at three pm. He mulled over his life in over last eighteen months. He'd lost count of the number of times he'd made this journey. His eccentric Uncle Arthur Sexton, Earl of Mayclew had left him Garantan, the rambling old house and estate on Co Mayo. Arthur was a bachelor and great grandson of the Earl who built the house on the four hundred acre estate. Peter was the closest relative to whom he could leave it. Peter had enjoyed visiting his uncle with his parents and liked him, but never expected to inherit Garantan.

* * *

"Lord Sexton, did you give Sean Cooney permission to drive your vehicle?" Chief Superintendent Daniel O'Riordan asked.

"Please, just call me Peter. Yes, as I told you I asked him to take the car for its MOT as I had to attend a meeting at Westminster."

"We have liaised with the London Metropolitan Police who have confirmed your presence in London on Monday evening and at the time of the shooting."

"I should hope so, I make no secret of my whereabouts," Peter snapped. "

"How long had Mr Cooney been in your employment?"

"It'll be a year next month. He was loyal and I trusted him. This is such a tragedy. I don't know how his wife Marie's going to cope," Peter replied, looking round the scuffed cream walls of the shabby interview room. O'Riordan waited. He knew from years of experience that his interviewee was about to open up. He looked at Sexton, a tall man in his forties, his accent so different to his own.

"Who would want to kill Sean? They thought it was me. I'm sure. I never thought he'd be at risk driving that bloody car. I'd put him on the insurance the day before so he could borrow it," Peter said.

"Why did you do that?"

"His wife has rheumatoid arthritis. She needs to use his car for hospital appointments and shopping in the village. Her car gave up. They couldn't afford to replace it," Peter replied.

"Why do you think it was you the killer wanted to murder?"

"I know I'm not popular with some people in the village, especially since I replaced the boundary fencing and repaired the walls. By the way, what happened to that man Ryan who attacked one

of my fencing contractors?"
"Aiden Ryan was given a six month suspended sentence. The victim suffered minor injuries but was badly shocked. Ryan maintained you moved the boundary half an acre into his land."

"My Solicitor has written to him. According to the property deeds that half acre is part of the estate. The fence may have been moved over the years."

"Do you think it was Ryan who fired the shot?"

*   *   *

"It could have been anyone. I've probably unintentionally stirred up old resentments. In my Uncle's latter years people were used to having the run of the place." "Thank you Lord Sexton. You may rest assured we'll do all we can to identify the killer. Will you be staying at the house? We'll need you to stay in the area."

"Yes, of course. You have my landline number. My mobile has patchy service here."

"I'm sorry for your loss."

"Thank you."

*   *   *

Peter felt a cold shiver when taxi driver told him the front entrance to the estate was cordoned off. Driving past the white taped crime scene, he saw in the beam of the headlights the words 'BRITS OUT' scrawled in dripping red paint on the newly rendered wall. He watched the tail lights of the taxi disappear through the overgrown bushes on the back avenue as he fumbled in his jacket pocket for the key to the huge oak door. Using the light of his mobile phone to find the keyhole he turned the key in the lock and pushed the door. The hall smelled musty and damp. Having felt for the light switch, he walked past the huge empty grate. This place feels so dismal he thought. How I miss Sean, he'd had the lights on, fires lit, and Marie would have stocked the fridge when I told them I was coming over. The poor woman, I'll go and see her at her daughter's place tomorrow. She could hardly speak when I phoned her.

*   *   *

He poured himself a large whiskey and sat in his uncle's old leather chair in the small sitting room. It was the only room warm enough to sit in during the winter with the log fire blazing. He looked at the dusty books on the shelves and felt a reproachful glare from the portraits of stern faced ancestors on the walls. Picking up the old fashioned telephone, he could almost hear his Uncle Arthur's thin voice asking when he was coming over to visit him. He must have been lonely, the old boy, living in here on his own till he was 90. Peter wished he had visited more often. He tried to remember stories Uncle Arthur told him about growing up at Garantan. Sean Cooney's brother and wife had run the house cared for him in his latter years.

*   *   *

Peter dialed the number and waited for a reply. "Geoffrey, Thank God you're in. I'm in deep shit," he said.

"What's up?" his younger brother enquired.

"I'm at Garantan. My caretaker Sean's been shot, driving my car. I think they meant to shoot me."

"Wow, you're going too fast. Who meant to shoot you?" Geoffrey asked

"Someone in the village," said Peter.

"What have you done to upset the good people of Newcliff? They were perfectly friendly last time I was over," Geoffrey said.

"It's no joke Geoff. All I did was re-fence the boundaries and repair the perimeter walls."

"And that's why they want to kill you?"

"Dear old Uncle Arthur let the house fall down around him and the fields and woodlands go to rack and ruin. I had to start somewhere. Make it private." Peter shouted.

"So now the people have lost their playground?" Geoffrey suggested.

"Also their source of firewood and rubbish dumping ground," Peter added.

"You should get out of there. It doesn't sound safe. Put in a new local manager. What are you planning to do with the place anyway? Right now it sounds like a millstone round your neck," Geoffrey said.

"I want to fix it up, run it as a boutique hotel, and stock the woods with pheasants for the shooting season. Rich Arabs enjoy all that. I want to employ local people, use local produce, and put something back into the community. I'm also considering creating children's play area and small park for public use." Peter announced.

"That's a great plan, sounds expensive though," Geoffrey mused.

"I'll have to get some backing, might sell a few acres of the Wiltshire estate. Land's at a premium now. We've a couple of paintings that could fetch a good price too. ."

"Peter! It's far too late at night to get into that subject. You be careful. Get the Police to provide you with protection. Must go now; good night."

"Night Geoff" Peter replied.

Thursday
Peter found the key to his uncle's secure gun cabinet and took out a shotgun. He found some cartridges and loaded it. Uncle Arthur looked after his gun, if nothing else, he thought as the mechanism slid easily into place. I'm not surprised; he'd need to, living here on his own. I'll feel safer walking my land with this, he thought. He wanted to view the crime scene in daylight. As he approached the white tape he left the shotgun against a tree.

"Good morning Sir, the Garda on duty said

"Good morning, any developments yet?" asked Peter as he looked at the old round stone gatepost with a chunk of its stones lying on the ground.

"Forensics are examining the car and the autopsy results should be available this afternoon," the Garda replied

"That's good, thank you," Peter said.

*   *   *

Niamh spooned the last mouthful of lunch into James's dribbling mouth, wiping his chin with a large bib. "Where will we go for your walk today pet?" she smiled at him and he rocked his head, trying to smile. "It's going to be round the hen house, round the yard and down the lane a bit. That's about it I'm afraid. No more woods," she said. He made a strange guttural sound and shook his head. She looked out the window at the new fence posts and barbed wire which replaced the old broken fence. A walk in the woods had been the highlight of James's day. He loved the sound of the rustling leaves, the shafts of light trickling though the tree tops and the birds flying past them when they kept very still. He loved the low winter sunlight coming through the bare branches. Niamh watched his face light up when she pushed his wheelchair into the woods.

* * *

Paul kicked off his boots at the back door and ruffled James's hair as he passed him.
"How are you two?" He asked.
"I'm pissed off because James can't have his walk in the woods," Niamh answered.
"I know love. I'll take you both in the car on Sunday to the forest park, he said, lifting the lid of a saucepan on the cooker.
"Yes, there's soup for lunch. That's fine. What am I supposed to do the rest of the week?"
"I'll help you when I can, but there's no chance now of getting help with the milking. Do you think that bastard Sexton has any idea what life's like for people like us," Paul complained.
"Of course he hasn't. Sure wasn't it his family who threw my great grandparents off the land? Didn't care how poor they were," Niamh said.
"Are you ok? You're shaking." Paul put his arms round his wife. Her sobbing body shook against his shoulder.
"You try looking after James twenty four seven with only three measly mornings off a week. All I can do is sell eggs. The foxes got three hens last night. Now we can't even go into our woods." Paul held her close, felt her heart thump against his chest and her deep gasps of breath as she cried. What can I say to her? He thought. Six years of fighting since James was born. We knew he wasn't right. How long did it take for the doctors to diagnose cerebral palsy and learning difficulties? What a fight we had to get Dr Mathers to request a place and transport to and from the Day Centre. It was always the same answer, limited resources or else you fund it

yourself. I know Niamh would like to do more on the farm.

*   *   *

Aiden Ryan sat on a scratched grey plastic chair. The poster hadn't changed since he last sat in the corridor of the Castlebar Garda Station, 'Family Liaisons Officer, Phone 949038212.' A corner of the yellowing paper curled off the wall. In the interview room he was surprised when Chief Inspector Daniel O'Riordan introduced himself. I'm not used to big fish like him, he thought. He sounds like a Dubliner, not from round here.

"Mr Ryan, let's get straight to the point. As you know, Sean Cooney was shot on Tuesday morning. Where were you between nine thirty and eleven on Tuesday morning?" O'Riordan asked.

"In town here at the cattle market. I sold four heifers."

"Do you have witnesses to verify that?" O'Riordan looked at Ryan's big hands, rough scarred skin and grimy fingernails.

"Yes, the auctioneer knows me well. I have the receipts. It'll be on the animals' passports too."

"Thank you. We'll check that out. Lord Sexton told me he thought the killer meant to kill him, not Sean Cooney. Do you know anything about this?"

"No. I might have said I'd like to kill him, but I didn't really mean it."

"Your feelings towards Lord Sexton are obviously very strong."

"Yes. I guess if you were a farmer you'd understand."

"Tell me," said O'Riordan, picturing his brother's large farm in Co Wicklow.

"My family's worked that land for generations. Tennant farmers, just about survived, saw others evicted. They got a grant and bought the farm after the Land Act, spent years paying off the rest. Now this, "Ryan's anger filled the room.

"Is half an acre worth you getting a criminal record?" O'Riordan asked.

"It's the principle of it all. The letter said the estate would be replacing and repairing the boundary fence. I wasn't ready for land being shaved off. Why does Sexton think he can just ride roughshod over people who have lived here all their lives?" Ryan roared.

"Lord Sexton told me his solicitor wrote to you setting out the land measurements drawn up in the deeds of the estate."

"Yeah, well I'll fight him in the Courts over that."

"Thank you Mr Ryan. No further questions at present," O'Riordan said. He watched the large man leave the room and felt the floor shake as he slammed the door.

* * *

In the incident room O'Riordan informed his team of the autopsy results showing that Cooney was shot with a 410 shotgun. The shot made a hole in the driver's window. Fifteen steel balls of shot were found in the victim's head, his face suffering multiple impact wounds. Time of death was recorded at ten thirty on Tuesday morning.

"The killer must have shot Cooney as he checked the traffic before turning left out the gate. That puts the killer on the right of the car about ten feet away, concealed in the bushes. Tuesday was such a wet morning, evidence was found of condensation on the driver's window. It must have obscured Cooney's features from the killer. Any footprints found?" He asked.

"No Sir, the marks show that the killer stood on plastic of some sort, refuse sacks maybe, then they removed them." Sergeant Kelly reported.

"Get the surrounding area searched, look for discarded bags and footprints," O'Riordan ordered. We've got to find that 410 shotgun," O'Riordan said.

"How did the killer know when to target Sexton, if he was their intended victim?" Detective sergeant Jones asked.

"Did anyone else know about the NCT, Or MOT as Peter Sexton calls it?" Kelly asked.

"Get onto the NCT Centre in Clifden, ask if they had any enquiries, said O'Riordan.

"What about Michael Mooney, Westcliff Autos, he sold him the car?" asked Kelly

"I've spoken to him. He said he liked doing business with Sexton. Sexton didn't mind taking the Ford although it was due the test in two months. Mooney said he was on his own at the time," O'Riordan replied.

*   *   *

"Sir, there's a call for you. It's Peter Sexton," the desk sergeant said. O'Riordan put the phone on speaker mode.

"Hello Chief Inspector, I've just been to see the Flannerys to say how sorry I was about Cooney and the shock they must have had living just opposite the main gate. They were friendly and said they were glad it wasn't the Gardai at the door again. They'd already told them they were out on Tuesday morning. They said they'd seen Paul Quinn paint 'Brits Out' on the wall on Monday night and felt terrible about it. They were looking for some grey paint to cover it over. Paul rents land from me. Just letting me know in case there's any relevance," Peter Sexton said.

"Thank you very much," O'Riordan said

"Get Quinn in here ASAP," O'Riordan demanded.

*   *   *

"Keep your hair on, I'm coming," Niamh complained. The loud knocking on the door had made her jump and James shrieked.

"Good evening Mrs Quinn. Is Paul Quinn here?" asked DS Jones.

"He's down in the yard, should have finished the milking. What do you want him for?" Niamh looked at the two Gardai.

"Thank you, we just need him to help with our enquiries," Sergeant Jones replied. Paul saw the two Gardai approach the yard and walked towards them.

"Paul Quinn?" Asked Jones.

"That's me. Can I help you?" Paul asked.

"We need you to come with us to the Garda station to answer a few questions," Said Sergeant Jones.

"I'll just go and take off my overalls and boots, keep the muck out of your car," Paul said, trying to appear nonchalant. Niamh opened the door expecting them all to come into the kitchen.

"You're taking him away?" She asked

"Just for routine enquiries," DS Jones said.

*   *   *

This is all we need Paul thought as he looked out the car window. At the Garda Station he was fingerprinted and ushered into the interview room.

"Mr Quinn, a witness saw you paint the slogan 'Brits Out' on the wall of the Garantan estate. You know this is a criminal offence?" O'Riordan asked.

"I was so fired up with anger. It was a stupid thing to do," Paul said, his face reddening.

"Where were you between ten and eleven on Tuesday morning?" O'Riordan asked. He watched Paul Quinn's face change from embarrassment to shock.

"I was at my brother's farm. We help each other with calving. A calf got stuck, breech I think. We had to get the vet in the end to get it out, thought we were going to lose the cow. You can check it out with them," Paul replied.

"We will. You can give details of their names and phones numbers later. Why were you so angry on Monday night?"

"I got a letter from the new landlord, Sexton. He's putting the rent up. I don't know how I'm going to manage. Things are tight already. This new fencing's cut us off from the woods we've walked in all our lives. We've a disabled son. He loves the trees. My wife took him for walks in the woods in his wheelchair every day. She says he's much harder to manage now," Paul said.

"That must be very difficult for you all but we have a murder here. We've checked on the database. You have a firearms certificate for a shotgun."

"Yes it's for my father's old 410 shotgun. I shoot the odd fox with it. They've taken enough of our hens."

"We need to see it now," O'Riordan said.

*   *   *

As he got out of the car, Paul heard James shrieking, he ran into the kitchen, two Gardai following. He reached up to a set of keys on a hook and held one of them out to DS Jones. "The gun cabinet's in the hall under the stairs. I have to find Niamh" He called as he ran to see if she was in the bathroom or the bedroom. James did not like to be left on his own. Paul ran outside shouting her name. He panicked. This was not like Niamh. He ran to the henhouse and down to the barn. He looked in horror. Niamh was hanging by a rope from a metal beam, her eyes bulging, her face blotched purple and red. A wooden stepladder lay on its side on the ground, a muddy pink slipper beside it. Paul couldn't move, couldn't scream. He just kept staring up. Sergeant Jones took his arm. He had checked that Niamh was already dead.

"Paul. Let's go to your son. Sorry but you can't help her now." Paul let himself be helped into the kitchen. He couldn't feel his legs. He tried to shut out the vision of Niamh hanging there, her legs dangling, told himself it wasn't true. He hugged James. Everything seemed to merge into a blur.

* * *

Outside the house Sergeant Jones phoned O'Riordan, "We've another body, Quinn's wife Niamh. Hanged. Can you get the team up here, Quinn and his son are in a in a bad way. ...Yes, we've got the 410 shotgun."

* * *

White suited forensics arrived. Paul and James were driven away by a female officer

Friday
O'Riordan called at Dermot Quinn's farm. Dermot's wife Jenny answered the door. "Morning Chief Inspector, I can't believe Niamh's gone. We're just numb, on auto pilot. Come in and have a seat. I'll get Paul," she said. O'Riordan watched Paul walk unsteadily into the room, his face pale, dark shadows round his eyes. They sat down.

"I'm very sorry to have to tell you that Niamh took her own life. There's no evidence of anyone else being involved," he said.

"Are you sure? Niamh loves James too much to do that." Paul said.

"Maybe she felt she couldn't cope. The only recent fingerprints on the ladder are hers."

"I just don't believe it," Paul said.

"It may be because she shot Sean Cooney thinking it was your landlord," O'Riordan said.

"What? How could you say that? My wife's not a murderer," Paul said.

"I'm sorry Paul. I know this is hard for you. We traced a call to the NCT Centre in Clifden. Two weeks ago a woman phoned from a public phone in Castlebar Shopping Centre saying she was Lord Sexton's secretary. She gave the car registration number and asked the date and time of his NCT. Sexton knew nothing of this."

"That doesn't prove it was Niamh," Paul said.

"We interviewed Michael Mooney at the garage. We had to jog his memory but he said Niamh asked him what Sexton was like. She asked what car he'd bought. Mooney told her it was four years old, due for its NCT in a month." O'Riordan said.

"We've been friends with the Mooneys for years. She was just chatting," Paul said.

"I'm afraid it was more than that. How else did she know when to expect Sexton to be in here in Westcliff and what time he'd be driving out his gate? Her fingerprints were on the shotgun as well as yours" O'Riordan asked.

Paul stared at the red roses and green leaves in the swirling patterned carpet. He felt dizzy James went to the Day Centre on Tuesday mornings. Niamh told him her father had taught her to shoot as a teenager.

"Niamh shot a fox last week. It got three of our three hens." Paul said.

*   *   *

"I'm sorry, Paul. I'll leave you now," O'Riordan said. Paul sat staring at the carpet.

"I'll see you out. I'm just about to take Paul to the Respite Care to see James," said Jenny as she opened the front door for O'Riordan.

Saturday

Extra chairs lined the aisle of the Chapel. Every seat was taken, people squashed into the pews, more people stood outside. Rain lashed onto a sea of umbrellas. Peter watched Paul and Dermot Quinn, and Aiden Flynn help carry Sean Cooney's coffin. At the graveside he shook Paul's hand.

"I'm so sorry about your wife. O'Riordan told me what happened. I'd have made a gate for her to take your son into the woods if I'd only known," he said. Paul did not answer.

Souvenirs
Lynda Collins

It had all started with a pint of milk. June had simply tucked it into the crook of her arm when she was paying for the rest of her groceries, forgotten about it and then accidently stolen it from the supermarket. It had been a busy day, exacerbated by cold rain and insistent wind, and she'd been exhausted and preoccupied. All that she'd wanted to do was to get home, get a shower and a cup of tea to warm herself up, and neither she or the gormless shop assistant had paid any attention to the extra item. It was an easy mistake to make, and it could have happened to anyone.

She'd been halfway down the street, struggling to zip up her coat against the bad weather when she had realised her mistake. She'd been so surprised she nearly dropped the milk. For a minute or two she just stood, stunned, on the pavement, wondering what on earth she should do about the offending item.

The moral part of her brain shouted at her that she should go back and pay for it, after all, it *was* technically stealing, and stealing was of course absolutely, positively wrong. But there was also another, louder part of her brain that pointed out that what she had just done had been very easy, and also, when you thought about it, just a little bit exciting.

She tucked the milk inside her bag and continued in the direction of her apartment.

When she finally made it home the cup of tea that she made did the job of warming her up, and the stolen milk made it taste just a little bit better than normal.

Two days later she went shopping again, feeling braver, and this time she stole intentionally: nothing expensive, just a cheap eye shadow from a display stand in a chemists. It wasn't a colour or brand that she would use, just a cheap, brightly-coloured makeup palette like something a young teenager might wear. She had no real reason to choose it; it was simply the first thing that she could slip into her bag without anyone noticing. Taking it gave her a rush she'd never experienced before.; she could feel her heart racing excitedly in her chest as she walked out of the shop.

In another shop, two doors down, she tried it again, leaving this time with a mass-produced, faux Ancient Egyptian artefact tucked inside her coat, and excitement burning in the pit of her stomach.

She was utterly hooked. It was a thrill that she wanted, *needed,* to experience again and again.

* * *

"Oh, I just can't decide," June gushed to the shop assistant. She was dressed in some of her favourite clothing; all expensive, all designer and every piece of it stolen within the last month. The only part of her outfit that she'd actually paid for was the hair band that kept her long blonde hair pulled back from her face. She held up two almost identically hideous silk scarves. "Which do you think would suit me better? I need a man's opinion."

The shop assistant was a young man, certainly no older than eighteen or nineteen, still suffering from teenage acne, with large ears and bad hair. She had been flirting outrageously with him leaving him stammering and clumsy, which was just how she wanted him.

"I, umm... I'm sure that either one would look good on you," he said blushing furiously.

"You think so?" she simpered, holding each of them up against her throat in turn. His eyes followed, hovering slightly on her cleavage as she'd planned; she'd worn a low cut top just for such a purpose. "Oh dear. I don't know, I'll have to think about it. I just- I had wanted a scarf with a bit more blue in it..."

He interrupted, as wide eyed and excited as a puppy. "There are some at the back of the store that are blue. I'll bring you some of them over."

She patted him on the arm and treated him to a grateful smile. "Oh, would you? How sweet of you."

He hurried to get the other scarves, and in the instant that his back was turned, she helped herself to various items of stock nearby. Two pairs of leather gloves, a few silk ties, a next year's diary covering in frolicking cats, and a pair of sunglasses with leopard print frames all went into her bag. She didn't need any of them, but that didn't matter, it was the act of stealing that was important not things that she actually brought home.

The young shop keeper returned his arms full of scarves,

wraps and even a few pashminas. "I brought a few different ones because I thought that you might-"

"I'm so sorry," she interrupted, her mask of politeness abandoned. "I've just had an important phone call and I have to go." She grabbed her bag and pulled her coat back on. "Thank you so much for all your help, you were an absolute star. If I can I'll come back later and take another look then."

"Oh, well, no problem," he said, looking disappointed. "Well, maybe later then."

As she exited the shop, she struggled not to laugh. It was just all so easy.

Over the last few months she'd developed all sorts of shoplifting techniques. For small items she tended to stuff them into big pockets or hide them inside baggy clothes. She actually had a coat that she'd sewn an extra pocket into the inside of the sleeve; perfect for slipping things inside when no one was around. On rainy days she would use a large umbrella which she could hang casually over her arm at the elbow, where a few things might 'accidently' fall inside. On a few occasions she'd stolen clothing by wearing it under her own clothes, timing her exit of the shop with other customers who had actually paid for their goods just in case she set the alarms off. Her favourite though, was the specially lined bag that she'd made with a tin foil which prevented most security alarms from going off. If anyone ever looked in her bag she'd never be able to justify it, but then who would ever suspect her?

Then there were the distraction techniques, like the one that she'd just used, which generally worked quite well, particularly where young men were involved. A new technique which she hadn't used much yet, but which she was enjoying trying out, was the 'brass neck' technique, which was best used for larger items. She'd stolen a TV from Tesco's like that, simply walking out with a TV in the trolley and an old receipt clamped between her teeth. People saw a well dressed lady, who clearly had a receipt and simply assumed that she'd bought and paid for it and thought nothing of it. Easy. Exciting.

She glanced down at her watch. Three o'clock. Plenty more time before the shops closed, and there was still lots of room in her bag. She looked around, pulled the newly acquired sunglasses from her bag and put them on, a small smile playing over her lips.

Now, what other shops were nearby?

*   *   *

It was ten o'clock on a Monday morning when June found herself rudely awakened by her maid pulling open the curtains to let the light in. She groaned, rolled over in bed and pulled her pillow over her eyes.

"What's all this rubbish?" snapped the maid in a voice that was sharp enough to cut diamonds.

June gingerly moved aside the pillow to see her maid, Helen, standing beside the ornate dressing table, her hands on her hips. The maid was a good twenty years older than June, probably in her mid-forties, judging by her grey hairs and the crow's feet around her eyes. She would have been about the same age as June's dearly departed mother and sometimes she seemed to think that gave her the authority to act as though that was who she was. Even from a distance June could feel the disapproval radiating off her maid in waves.

"Don't touch them," June snapped, sitting up and throwing back the covers, "they're mine."

She felt an inexplicable surge of possessiveness rush through her. The assorted items on the table might have seemed like a random collection of the most obscure and gaudy of knickknacks but to June they were souvenirs, trophies. Some were old, amongst the first few things that she'd stolen, and some of them were brand new. Yes, the ceramic figurines, purses, keyrings, money boxes and other bits and pieces might have seemed out of place on the Georgian oak dresser, but every time she looked at them, or held them in her hands —even now—she felt an echo of the same thrill she'd had the moment that she had when she'd walked out of the shop without paying for them. She wouldn't have considered buying any one of them, but stealing them? Now that, that was different.

Helen's lips twisted disapprovingly, "you've been at it again, haven't you?" She shook her head and stepped away from the evidence as though she thought that standing this close to them would incriminate her. "I don't understand it. You're rich, in fact you're loaded. You could buy the shops and their entire contents three times over, yet you're addicted to stealing this... tat from them."

Swinging her legs out of bed, June padded across her

bedroom floor, coming to stand closer to her most recent acquisitions. "It's not owning them that's important, it's *taking* them. If you've never done it," she tried to explain, "you just can't understand, I wouldn't expect you to. Stealing... it's just so exciting. It just gives me such an adrenalin rush. It's like nothing else you could ever imagine."

Her maid shook her head. "That may well be, though personally I still don't understand. All I know is that someday you'll end up getting caught, and when your father gets word of that you'll be in all sorts of trouble. It'll be in all the papers. I'll probably get the sack, you'll be disgraced, and your father's career could be ruined."

June's temper flared. "I doubt he'd bat an eyelid, besides, I'm sure that he has a few skeletons in his closet too. He's not exactly the squeaky clean businessman that he'd like you to believe that he is."

"Can't you at least store them away somewhere?" The maid tutted at the stolen objects as though they were an affront to her. "Somewhere out of sight?"

"Ok. Here," June's frayed temper snapped. She took the platinum account card from her purse and thrust it rudely into her maid's hand. "If they're such an affront to you, go and buy a box for them. Then you won't have to look at them anymore."

* * *

The next day June was out driving in her new softop BMW. It had been a recent present from her father after he'd completed a particularly lucrative business deal. It was a nice enough car, but she was a little annoyed about the whole thing; she had specified that she'd wanted it in purple, not blue. It would do, for now. She was passing through the outskirts of the city centre, in the old part of town where the tyres of her car made a strange ticking rhythm on the stones of the cobbled streets.

She liked it here; this was a rich hunting ground for her, an upper class part of town full of small boutiques and jewellery shops packed with lots of lovely things that her fingers itched to touch and to take, and what was better, the shops generally didn't have the security systems of the larger stores meaning she was less likely to get caught.

There was a shop nearby that she wanted to visit. She'd

passed it a few days ago and the window display had called to her. Unfortunately, it had been closed then, but today as she drove past, she'd noticed the sign in the window was turned to say, "We're open. Come on in."

June didn't need to be asked twice.

Pulling the vehicle into the first empty space she could find, she paused in the car to adjust her makeup. She checked herself in the mirror and blew a kiss to her reflection. She'd do.

She lifted her bag from the seat beside and tested its weight. There was a science to stealing that she'd learned over the last few months. For example, she'd learned that you should carry a large bag, but not too big—you don't want to accidently knock things over and draw attention to yourself—and you wanted it to be relatively full to give it some weight, but no so full as to leave no room for something that you suddenly wanted to have. She always coupled the large bag with a large purse as it could be used to shield your actions from view, and could be quickly moved to cover whatever new possession you might have just slipped into your bag. Her pulse accelerated in anticipation as she stepped out of her car.

June walked down the street, past the delicatessens, organic vegetable shops and artisan bakeries that seemed to breed in this part of town, past numerous coffee shops and cafes and high-class charity shops that sold designer clothes. Outside a master butcher's a man offered her a free sample of their 'sausage of the month' but she declined. It was no fun to be offered things for free after all; it was only fun if she helped herself without anyone noticing.

Finally, she made it to the shop that she'd been aiming for. June paused outside, looking in the window. It was a small independent shop that sold household goods: things like fancy crockery and cast-iron cooking pots, ergonomic composters and garden tools sets, as well as local arts and crafts and a host of other miscellanea.

For a moment she paused to settle her nerves, but the desire to steal something, anything, was too strong. Her hands were shaking with anticipation as they reached for the door.

The shop doorbell rang brightly as she entered. Behind the counter sat a middle-aged man, with thinning, sandy hair and wire-framed glasses. He looked up from his newspaper when she came in, smiled and then returned his eyes to the crossword in front of him.

June smiled to herself. He might has well have just told her to help herself.

She wandered around the shop, running her hands over the furniture and touching anything that caught her eye. She was pretending to browse, but in reality she was scouting for something to take. There was so much that she wanted to steal, but she had to be careful, if she were to take too much she'd be bound to draw attention to herself.

Finally her eyes rested on a little ceramic bowl on a shelf amongst other wheel-thrown pottery. It was cheap and gaudy-looking, covered in brightly-coloured swirls and loops as though the potter who'd made it had been high at the time. That didn't matter to June; she simply needed to have it. Her fingers closed on it, and when she knew that the shopkeeper wasn't looking she swiftly slipped it inside her coat.

The rush of adrenalin was instant and intoxicating, like she'd just taken a fast-acting drug. She felt heady and invincible and a little turned on.

She turned and headed for the door.

"Ten pounds fifty," said a voice from behind the counter. She froze and turned around to see the shopkeeper was looking right at her.

"What do you mean?" she asked innocently.

"For the bowl. I was watching you admire it on CCTV." The extra emphasis that he put on the word 'admire' made it quite clear what he had seen her do.

She stared at him for a moment, trying to decide what to do. She could own up, pretend that it had all been an accident, or she could she try and call his bluff? Her heart was racing again, but it wasn't excitement this time. "Fine," she said, finally, deciding that it was safer to comply. She handed him her platinum credit card. "Charge it to that."

The shopkeeper swiped the card, and waited a few seconds for it to clear. After a moment the machine beeped in a way that June had never heard before. "It's been rejected," he said bluntly. "Have you got another one?"

Her eyebrows shot up. "Rejected? That's impossible."

He gave her an impatient look, "and yet, it's happened," he grunted.

She gave him a different card. It was rejected too. As were her other three.

"Looks like I'll have to phone the police then," said the storekeeper firmly.

"Wait. There's clearly been some sort of banking error or something." An image of her father's face when he heard that she'd been arrested flashed through her mind

"I'm sure I have it here somewhere." She rummaged through her purse, and then her bag and found just enough cash to pay.

"Have a nice day," he told her, handing over a receipt. "Please don't come again."

June snatched the piece of paper and left the shop with a burning face. She'd never been so embarrassed in her life, she wanted the ground to open and swallow her. She practically ran back to her car, flinging her bag onto the passenger's seat, not giving a damn as to whether the stupid plate survived or not.

The BMW's tyres screeched on the road as she sped away. She needed to put some distance between her and the shop, and she also needed to phone the bank and find out what was wrong with her cards. There must have been some sort misunderstanding or something. There was no way that they should have been rejected, not considering the upper limits that they had on them.

* * *

Letting herself into her luxury flat, it took less than a second to tell that something was badly wrong. The hallway was dark, echoing and totally empty. She'd been robbed.

She walked, stunned, through the corridors, her high-heels echoing on the bare marble floors. The walls had been stripped of all of her carefully chosen art, the expensive Persian rugs had been taken from the floors and every stick of furniture was missing. It looked as though no one lived here at all. The thieves had gone through it with a thoroughness that quite took her breath away. They'd left her with nothing.

Well, not quite every nothing. When she made it to what had been her bedroom, there was a box sitting alone on the floor in the middle of the room. Inside it were her souvenirs, some bank and credit card statements printed that day, using an awful lot of red ink

and a six word note written in her maid's handwriting.
> June lifted it with shaking fingers.
> *You were right.* It said simply. *Stealing is fun.*

"Skeletons In The Closet"

"That's her. Number two."

The Spirit: A Tale of Misdirection
Ellie Rose McKee

The truck's breaks made a squeaking sound as it pulled to a halt outside the large, electrified gates of *The Taskforce*'s headquarters. Rolling down the window, the driver gave a nod to the female security guard. Her eyes drifted to the backseat momentarily, she gulped and pressed the button to put a call through directly to the main building atop the hill. Within moments a gruff voice echoed around her little hut in response.

"What is it?" it said.

"Johnson has returned from his patrol," said the security guard, glancing back at the driver, "Looks like he's found something."

The man on speakerphone was silent for a moment, before letting out a sigh. "I'll call everyone together. Get him to bring whatever it is up to us. Oh, and order some coffee. You know how long these meetings can stretch on for."

"Yes sir," she said before pressing the button again, to cut off the call. Returning her eyes to Johnson she whispered, "I hope this works."

"It will," he reassured her, reaching forward to give her hand a squeeze, "It has to."

She opened her mouth to speak again, but he took back his hand and shook his head at her before she could get any words out. "Don't say it. I already know. And you don't need to tell me to take care either. It'll be okay. We'll make it through this, you'll see."

Her shoulders dropped in resignation, and she turned to face away from him and pull down the lever - raising the barrier, allowing him a clear entry to the compound.

"Better get up there then," she said, in as even a tone as she could manage; refusing to face him again.

* * *

Inside the boardroom the four core members of The Taskforce took their seats alongside the two Council Chiefs. Johnson was last to enter, carrying a body bag over his shoulder.

Slowly, he lowered it to the floor and unzipped it as everyone leaned forward to see the occupant. There were a few gasps around the room as they all recognized her instantly – despite the vast damage to her body. It was riddled with bullet holes and covered in blood from the neck down, but her face was intact and her eyes were open; seemingly looking straight through them.

The owner of the gruff voice – Taskforce Leader Number One, Adam Hanch – stood up and looked at Johnson. "You do this?" he asked.

"No," said Johnson, "You did."

Again there were a couple of shocked inhalations of breath but no-one else dared say anything.

"And just what in the hell is that supposed to mean?" snapped Hanch.

The young man didn't answer. Instead he opened his coat and pulled something from the inside pocket. Upon setting it on the table and sliding it across to Council Chief Madison Jacks, it became obvious they were all looking at a DVD box.

"Watch it," said Johnson; leaving the room before they could demand further explanation.

Taskforce Leader Four - Lucille Jacks, the main Council Chief's wife – started to stand up, ready to yell after him for exiting without permission, but Hanch put a firm hand on her shoulder and she shrank back into her seat.

"Get the AV team to hook it up to the main screen," he said, to no-one in particular. Lucille nodded and took the task upon herself.

* * *

The group found themselves staring up at an image of the deceased woman, who was still laid out on the floor in front of them: Bernie

Jenkins, political activist and thorn in their proverbial side for a number of years. On screen she was wearing the same outfit as she had on now but most importantly, on screen she was still living and breathing. Slowly the realization dawned on each of them, that the video had only been recorded mere hours ago. After a moment or two the still image sprung to life and her voice boomed out into the room.

"I'm assuming everyone I need is here, watching me," she said. "Protocol dictates that you are, and if there's anything I've learnt in the past couple of years, it's that you take protocol very seriously."

Turning her head to the left, she directed her eyes to where Hanch sat. He knew she couldn't see him, of course, but that didn't make him feel any less uncomfortable. Truth was that protocol dictated a lot more than who would be in the room: it outlined specifically which room they would be using and in which order they were sat. It was a clever tactic, to manipulate protocol, and she excelled at. Part of him had to admire her for that, grudgingly.

* * *

"First of all," she continued, "I guess I should say congratulations. You finally got what you wanted. There's no chance of me messing up your pretty little plans now, is there?"

The gleam in her eye was testament to the fact she knew all too well that it wasn't true. Her death – the thing they had sought for quite some time – was meant to screw up everything they'd worked for. They just didn't know how, yet.

"Secondly, if you don't mind, I'd like to take you on a history lesson. But don't worry, I'll be brief." The gleam in her eyes vanished and her shoulders tensed as she moved her eyes left to right, seemingly scanning the room. "You are a powerful force – individually and collectively. When we rebuilt society from the ground up, putting you in charge seemed like the obvious choice. You were the champions we stood behind in the war. You're the reason we won. But with the threat of mass nuclear warfare removed, and nothing but power to occupy you, it was pitiful how quickly things changed. Suddenly protecting that power, regardless of cost, was the highest priority. And who could blame you? You earned it, no-one had any right to threaten it. Is that was you tell yourselves at night, when you can't sleep for thoughts of the blood on your hands?"

Some of the group hung their heads at that, giving credence to her words, but Hanch's face remained resolute.

"Do you keep a count of how many people you've executed for standing up against your régime? I tried compiling a list, once, in the hopes on honoring the dead once you'd been toppled. But the list grew too long, and you showed no signs of disbanding any time soon. Suddenly I knew I needed to step up my game if I was to set things straight. Democracy in our nation had all but died, but I knew true power still lay with the people. All I had to do was get the right ones on board to put pressure in necessary places."

Hanch slammed his fist on the desk before rising to his feet and beginning to pace back and forth. The rest of the group looked at him for a moment, but when it became obvious he was still intent on listening to the rest of the video their attention returned to it, with only a few glances down at the body before doing so.

"When all you're interested in is power, and protecting it," she said, "It's amazing what you'll neglect. Such as your children."
The eyes focused on her image widened at the implication and the air grew increasingly thick with tension. Each person at the table had at least one child. Lucille and Madison Jacks had four, between them, so it was unsurprising that they appeared the most nervous.

"It barely took any convincing at all to get them on board. In fact, when I explained the plan they practically begged me to let them help. How does that make you feel? When you lose your own flesh and blood in the name of your agenda? I'll tell you, shall I? It's the worst thing in the world. Do you remember that time you shot my son in cold blood, thinking it would scare me into giving up exposing you for what you really are?" She let out a short, joyless, laugh. "Guess that backfired for you. See, when you lose everything, there's nothing left to hold you back. Funny thing is, if you hadn't of done it I wouldn't have been able to do enact this plan now. Maybe that'll keep you up tonight, if the blood doesn't."

"Bitch!" shouted Hanch, who had stopped pacing to stand facing forward again. With fists clenched he bit back everything else he was wanting to shout at her; knowing it to be futile. Knowing she'd finally won.

*   *   *

"So, ladies and gents, here's the plan. You either hand in your resignations and set up a fair election to find your replacements – insuring it really is fair – or you stay put and change back the legislation to what it should have been all along; banning executions for crimes of 'Threats to the Taskforce', stopping censorship of the media, reinstating some form of third party organization to monitor internal affairs, that sort of thing.

"You should be lucky I'm giving you a choice at all, really. It was more than your brats were willing to provide you. Hell, if they had their way I'm sure they'd have banded together to have you hung drawn and quartered. Literally."

Lucille let out a little whimper at that, and looked towards her husband for comfort but he refused to meet her gaze. Eventually she looked back at Bernie, who's eyes where now aimed directly at her.

"I want you to know just how much they hate you. For not being around much as they grew up, for the bullying they received for many years because of who their folks were, and mostly for having to live with the fact their mummies and daddies were off unashamedly killing people each and every day to keep them in the manner to which they'd become accustomed.

"I'm sure you rationalized it internally, with time. Told yourself it was necessary to stop dissention in the ranks; that it was all for the greater good. But it's not so easy to pull the wool over the eyes of your little ones. Trust me, I know. My boy came to me the day before he died; sat me down and told me I was on a suicide mission. Those were his exact words, can you imagine? All very ironic now, isn't it? But he was right, and I told him as much. No matter how important the cause I was fighting was, it wasn't worth risking my life, or putting him through losing me. Not after he'd already had to go through letting go of his dad at such a young age. And so I promised him I'd stop; that I'd let someone else try and put an end to your corruption. I was just about ready to wave my white flag when his body appeared on my doorstep. So, as I've said, you're plan really did backfire."

* * *

The video stopped, then, and they all looked around to see the door open. Johnson walked back into the room carrying a tray with mugs on it. "Thought I'd bring in the coffee you ordered before playing part two," he said.

Hanch took hold of him and the tray dropped to the ground, causing its contents to smash everywhere. Some bits of ceramic clung to the corpse.

"You think this is a game?!" he spat, before feeling a tight grip across his own arms.

"Put him down, Adam," said the man behind him – Taskforce Leader Three: Jerry Montero – "Don't you think we've done enough damage?"

But Hanch was too overcome with fury to listen. He pulled away from Jerry and pinned the soldier to the wall before putting his hands round his throat. Number three punched Hanch in response; knocking him to the ground before looking back up at Johnson.

"Get someone to put him in the hole until he calms down," he commanded him. "We'll finish the rest of the meeting without him."

Johnson nodded, both in agreement and in thanks, before once again turning to leave. Jerry spoke out again, though, momentarily stopping him in his tracks saying, "Whatever the outcome of this meeting, we will investigate your involvement in orchestrating it and punishments will be doled out; you have my word."

Johnson's face hardened, but he did not respond.

*   *   *

When Hanch's unconscious body had been removed from them, the group returned to their seats and someone in the AV room behind them pressed play on part two. Instantly the wall danced again with color and their eyes were drawn back to an image of Bernie's face. She was a striking woman, with sharp features that suited her face as well as her personality. She was in her late thirties but both sounded and looked younger, yet certainly not immature. Commanding a certain respect, even from those opposed to her, she had always been a force to be reckoned with. It should have been no surprise that she would take the hard way out.

"You're probably wondering how *exactly* I ended up dead, in front of you."

Again eyes from around the room flitted to her body as she took a momentary pause.

"Well, it's kind of complicated; in a bit of a grey area between suicide and murder. So sorry about that. I know how much you hate grey areas. That's why you ditched the whole '*To Protect and Serve*' motto so early on, right? Because justice is too complex a thing to grapple with. It's much easier to stick focus on convicting people according to generic rules that can be so easily changed at a moment's notice, rather than take inconvenient circumstances into account. Much easier to calm your conscience when you get to decide what's right and wrong, I imagine.

"I don't need to tell you how ridiculous I find your system. Or indeed how problematic you're now likely considering it to be yourself, now that you're on this side of it. But, again, I'm gonna give you a choice in how to deal with this problematic matter. You can stick to your guns and keep protocol as it currently stands, meaning you *will* have to resolve my loss of life one way or the other; you could posthumously convict me of the crime of suicide, you could convict each of your offspring for their hand in my death, you could even convict yourself for driving me to it, but the other option, of course, is to change the laws so as none of those things happen and some semblance of justice prevails. That's the one I'm gunning for, so to speak. Did anyone ever teach you about the spirit of the law being more important than the actual specifics themselves? I'm guessing not, but I'm also guessing I've lost you somewhat. I'd put money on the fact that right about now you're sat there, distracted by the fact I said your kids caused my untimely demise. Part of you doesn't want to believe it's true, but somewhere in the back of your skull you know I'm not lying. You can't think straight, until I put your minds at ease by telling you *how much* of a hand they had in it and gain some understanding of how difficult it'll be for you to wriggle them out of it.

"So here goes, this is how it *all* went down: I recorded this message, stepped into the little courtyard behind the room I'm I now, your darling children circled me, holding a gun in each hands – from your own armory, no less – and on the count of three they fired, simultaneously. That was to make sure you couldn't pick a scapegoat among your brood, on which to pin it all on so the rest could be absolved. Clever, don't you think?" she smiled, happy in her own plans. "They won't let you cover it up and have them all walk free either, you know?" she continued. "If you do nothing in light of my death they have all vowed, of their own accord, to follow in my footsteps and say goodbye to this world. Goodbye to everything you've worked so hard for. You cannot sweep this under the rug.

"I'll ask you again: how does it make you feel? And, more importantly, what will you decide? You've got two hours from the end of this message to make up your minds. Otherwise, you know what'll happen. If you can't agree, then come to some other arrangement to decide. I've heard there's this thing called democracy. Perhaps you could look it up, and give it a go."

She stopped speaking, but the tape did not end there. The

group sat and watched as she took a moment to stare down the lens at them. Finally she stood up, in front of the camera, and made her way to the door; turning back towards them just before placing her palm on the handle. All sarcasm and anger was gone from her. Her last words were quiet. Solemn.

"If this somehow doesn't work. If by some miracle you find a way to get around dealing with my death and avoiding the suicides of your offspring without having to relinquish control of the state; and if all my death achieves is that I won't have to be around to witness such a further corruption of policy then I won't regret this. I can't continue to live in a world where everything is so toxic. Question is: can you?"

There was another pause.

"Please make things right," she said, earnestly pleading with each one of them. All pretense dropped. "Please."

She looked at her feet, then pushed the handle the rest of the way down, opened the door and walked through it. There were a few more minutes of silence, then deafening noise, then the sound of the camera clicking off.

When the screen went black and the lights came up Lucille was screaming and crying uncontrollably. Madison walked over to Bernie's body and closed her eyes.

"Okay, folks," he said. "I think this is where the real meeting starts."

Unsolved
Ellie Rose McKee

It was a media frenzy, outside Dorset police headquarters. The car park had been full of paparazzi ever since the body of thirty-one year old Teresa Evans was discovered, just over two weeks ago. It had been a rough fortnight – for everyone. The world's eyes were on this small branch of law enforcement, expecting them to catch the brutal killer of a heavily pregnant woman. Mother to four other children. Founding member of the local PTA. Pillar of the community.
Today the bosses in London where looking to put an end to the spotlight, by bringing in 'the big guns': the leading homicide detective from across the pond, who was previously one of their own - Samantha Collins.

*   *   *

Patrick Stevens, who was the chief lead on the case, was pacing his disorderly office, waiting for her arrival. It was no secret that he didn't want outside help, but it was also well known that he had no choice. People had been avoiding him all day, lest they incur his misplaced wrath. When Samantha finally walked in his door, three hours late, he had been up for seventy six straight hours.

"Good grief!" she exclaimed, taking in his unkempt appearance. "First things first. We're getting out of this precinct to get you some hot food and a coffee."

"That's not what you're here for," he said, in an attempt to dismiss her.

"I am here to solve your case, and you are expected to help me. A little bit of civility and perhaps even gratitude wouldn't be uncalled for but, that aside, you're gonna need a clear head if we're to go through this so it's essential we take care of you. Don't make it any harder than it needs to be, Pat."

"Of course," he said, "It's all about the case. Should have

known you wouldn't want to take care of me simply because you actually care."

She shut the door then – shut out everyone in the outer office's not so subtle attempts at eavesdropping.

"I mean it, Pat. I'm not trying to make this difficult," she said in a softer tone while opening the blinds. He winced at the sudden brightness of the room and she took a better look at him. "Have you been drinking?"

"You don't want things to be difficult? Fine, then let's keep conversation to the case and not ask personal questions." There was a bitterness to his words, and she was tempted to challenge him but thought better of it. When she said nothing he continued, "You don't get to enquire after my well being and I won't ask for details of your perfect little life, since you left me for the sunny beaches of California and the waiting arms of whatever hunk you've got this week." Again she bit her tongue, as she threw his coat at him and reopened the door. Walking out, knowing he'd follow despite himself.

* * *

They got a small corner booth in a pub three towns over, to get away from any reporters who might think of following them. She ordered his food for him – a large burger and potato wedges – and a salad for herself, but both plates sat untouched in front of them.

"The gloom of this place doesn't take long to set back in, does it?" she said, and he glared at her, wearily. "Right, okay. No small talk as well as no personal questions." She sighed. "Tell me about the case."

Now it was his turn to sigh. "You already know all the details. No doubt you'll have gone through the case file sixteen times during the flight. I have nothing else to add."

"Humor me," she said. "Start from the beginning. What time was she found?"

"Seven thirty a.m. by a dog walker. As it says on page two."

"Sexually assaulted?"

He shook his head. "Not as far as we could tell."

"And the body was found in the woods, right? Any thoughts on how she got there? It's on the other side of town to her house."

"We're assuming the killer drove her there. Who, or why, that's anyone's guess."

Frustrated, she clenched her fists. "There must be more to this. There were no shoeprints found on scene?"

He shrugged. "Inconclusive."

She took a deep breath, asking, "How are the kids?"

"Do you mean the twins or the other ones?"

"The surviving twin," she confirmed.

"She's in intensive care. The doctors don't think she'll pull through."

"God!" she exclaimed, pushing her hands through her hair. "This is awful. I don't get it though. The coffin birth thing. Explain it."

"Samantha," he said, taking on a small air of professionalism; letting go of his initial aversions to having her work with him again. "This really is all in the report."

"The report says that after the woman died she gave birth. That when her body was found, one of the twins was dead and one was barely breathing. It does *not* explain to me how all that is possible."

"Coffin birth – or postmortem fetal extrusion, as it's also known – is very rare. It involves the decomposing body of a pregnant woman expelling the child. Due to the buildup gasses and-"

Samantha held up a hand, stopping his explanation mid sentence.

"What? Thought you wanted to know. You never were the squeamish type."

"There's a limit to everything," she stated, simply, before continuing. "As rare as this phenomenon is, I take it it's even less common for an expelled child to survive?"

He nodded and slumped his shoulders before reaching forward to pick up a potato wedge. "The circumstances would have to be precise. The body would have had to have been there long enough to build up enough of the gasses, but the child would need to have been found almost immediately after to stand even a tiny chance. I mean, it's a miracle that it would have even survived long enough to see the outside of the womb. The pregnancy would have to be in the extremely late stages, which it was. Even then... no-one could have predicted this."

She made an indignant noise. "Some miracle. What happens if the baby does survive, and doesn't have brain damage? I know it's unlikely, but as we've just covered, all of this is against the odds. Just think about it. If that little girl grows up, what kind of life will she have? I can see why the case is getting to you."

Now he grunted, saying, "You have no idea." And she glanced at him suspiciously.

"Is there something you're not telling me?"

He averted her gaze, then, and she laid a hand on his arm. "What is it?"

Defensively he pulled back his arm, before standing up, professionalism quickly taking a back seat again. "It is nothing. We know nothing else. The case is unsolvable. Put that in your report when you get back home."

* * *

When he stormed out of the pub it took Samantha a moment to follow, but when she did he was there, waiting for her in the car – engine revving. She got in, but he didn't drive. Silence filled the car. The tension built for a while until he snapped the key to the off position in the ignition and rested his head on the steering wheel.

Resisting the urge to place a comforting hand on his back, Samantha waited for him to do something else. Eventually he raised his head again and looked at her.

"Can I take you somewhere private?" he asked and she nodded.

* * *

They arrived at a bed and breakfast, a couple of streets away from the pub, and he paid up front for the full day. When they entered the room she turned to face him, folding her arms across her chest. "What is this all about, Pat?"

He walked past her, to take a seat on the edge of the bed. "You were right," he said. "There is more to the case."

Her body language changed at his admission, and she sat down in a chair facing him.

"If I tell you everything, do you promise to listen to it all before saying anything?" he asked, and she took a gulp of air before agreeing, against her better judgment.

* * *

Patrick's explanation began with him asking if she still remembered Mark Hollows. Whatever she'd been expecting, it wasn't that.

"I do," she confirmed.

"He became headmaster of our old high school six months ago. Was making a great job of it. Impressing everyone."

"Okay?" she said, not needing to add *'but what has that got to do with anything?'*

"He killed himself. Shot himself in the head, Wednesday morning."

"The same day Teresa was found?" she asked, already knowing the answer.

"Would have made front page news, if Teresa wasn't already taking it up. Her story blew everything else out of the water. As it was he got a one sentence mention, half way down the local obituary column."

"Would explain why I never heard," said Samantha, calmly, trying to hide her growing impatience with Patrick reaching some kind of conclusion.

"I was working Teresa's case when they pulled me off it,

temporarily, to go and take a peek at his. The first officers on scene found a sealed envelope next to his body, with my name on it. Inside there was a full confession."

"Confession? What... for Teresa's murder?" she stood up again, urgently, "Why haven't you reported this?!"

Patrick blocked Samantha as she made her way to the door, reminding her that she'd promised to hear everything first. After a moment or two she relented and sat, again. This time perched more forward, in expectation of something that would make it all better.

"The letter said that he had been having an affair with Teresa, on and off for years, since long before she got married. It went on to say that on the day she died she'd requested he pick her up and take her to their usual spot, in the woods. To talk, she said, apparently. When Teresa got him out there she told him he was the father of her twins. He was shocked, as you'd expect. He claims she'd always assured him, emphatically, that her husband was the dad until then. So he began to question her, and it became clear that it wasn't just the twins that belonged to him."

This information wasn't making Samantha feel any better. Again she felt the urge to report it all to her superiors, immediately, but she waited for the rest as she said she would.

"He says she wanted to tell him before she told everyone else. She was planning to expose their affair and the parentage of her children publicly."

"So he murdered her, before she could," Samantha concluded. "But that doesn't make sense, why would he then confess it."

"Mark said it was an accident – her death. That she was pacing as they spoke, getting more and more worked up, and he reached out to calm her but she pulled away sharply and tripped on a tree stump. Hit her head on a rock."

Samantha shook her head, struggling to take it all in. "You believe him?"

"I don't know," Patrick admitted, "But I don't think it matters what I believe."

"What do you mean? Of course it matters. It's pivotal to the case whether his confession is accurate or not."

"Oh, screw the case!" Patrick blurted, and Sam was notably shocked at the outburst. Knowing there must be some reason, for his unwillingness to investigate the confession properly she decided not to challenge him on it. He said he'd explain all, if she let him.

"Okay," she said, as much to herself as to him. "I'm trying to process this. Did Mark say anything about why she wanted to tell the world about their affair?"

"He didn't," said Patrick. "He said she told him he was the father of her twins, and in fact likely to have fathered all her children, then she told him she was going to make the news known to everyone, then the tripped over, in her agitated state, and when he checked her pulse he realized she wasn't breathing."

"So he just left her there?"

"Yes."

"Okay," said Samantha again. "What else?"

"In Mark's letter he said he went from the scene of her death to a local bar where he got drunk and stumbled home not long after closing time. The next day, when he sobered up, he wrote everything down."

"And then he shot himself," she finished the sentence for him.

"Yes."

"When are we going to get to the point where you explain why you're hiding this from the inspector?"

"Isn't it obvious?" said Patrick and from the look Samantha gave him in return he came to understand that it was not.

"If what Mark says is true then the line between it being a case of accidental death or manslaughter are a little unclear. It could be argued that she wouldn't have died if he hadn't reached out to calm her, but we also have to consider that reaching out is not an intentional act to harm someone. Regardless of that, he felt that he couldn't live with himself – hence the suicide. That leaves us with the fact that Teresa is dead, and Mark is dead and Teresa's husband pretty much had a breakdown when my officers broke the news to him. Dragging this into public doesn't change any of that. Mark knew that, but he also knew that it might be unavoidable. You can cut this several different ways, and you could call him a lot of things but I honestly believe that when he decided to explain everything and put the decision in my hands weather to reveal it or not, he had his children's best interests at heart. He wasn't stupid in some respects – he knew that all of this coming out wouldn't bring Teresa back, and more importantly he knew it would likely lead to his children being separated from the man they had grown up with. The truth would shatter an already grieving family. In fact, it may even stop them from being able to grieve for their mother properly. All in all it just leaves one hell of a messy situation and he didn't even know there was a chance one of the twins could survive. That makes it even more messy. And messier yet, he didn't know practically every news station in the world would jump on the story. Samantha, if we report the contents of that letter officially then no matter where those kids go for the rest of their lives they'll be infamous. The eldest is barely ten years old! I can't see a single good thing coming from putting it out there."

"But," said Samantha, tentatively, "What about bad things coming from keeping quiet?"

Patrick looked at her, unsure of what things she meant exactly.

"Hypothetically," she said, continuing, "If we don't say anything, but somebody later finds out some way or other we'd lose our entire careers for nothing. I know that shouldn't be our priority, but it should be considered as a factor. And what if we keep quiet but we can't handle it? Secrecy destroys people, Pat, we both know that more than most. Just look at you. You've been battling this for two weeks and quite frankly you look like hell, what's a year or a decade going to do you? Deciding here and now to say nothing may be a simple decision but it's one we'll both have to live with for a very long time. Are you sure you can do that? Because, if I'm honest, I'm not sure I can. And I do hear what you're saying. And I don't know if you're right about Mark thinking about what's best for his kids but I know *you* genuinely care and you are trying to do what's right. When we signed up to be part of law enforcement having these kinds of decisions resting on us was never supposed to be part of the deal. Law enforcement, think about those words. Our jobs are to do things by the book, because we trust that the book is based on justice, or on as much justice as anything man made can be. We're not supposed to enforce the laws we agree with and ignore the rest. If everyone did that where would justice be?"

"That's great," he said. "All of that makes sense, in theory, but in practice there are four, maybe five kids gonna be walking this earth – orphaned. Do you really think the guy that's brought them up so far will want to keep them even if social services let him? I can't have that on my conscious, Samantha. It may not be "just", but I believe it is *right* to at least give them some opportunity to avoid the brunt of this. You're right, the truth coming out anyway is a risk, but if *we* let it out it is a certainty.

"If you decide to follow this up, by the book, then I won't hold it against you. I'll go along with your decision. But if you think you can live with keeping the truth hidden, for the sake of the little ones, then I'll write my report stating it was an accidental death in circumstances unknown, and get you to agree with that finding - in court, if need be – either way, I'm done. I can't do this job anymore."

* * *

It was a long while, after Patrick finished speaking, that Samantha made up her mind. They sat there for near an hour in silence, not looking at each other, when she finally spoke.

"You're a good man, Patrick Stevens. You write your report, as you see fit, and I'll sign it off; concurring that my findings match yours when I receive a copy on my desk, come Monday morning. I'm not gonna prolong staying here; I don't think it's wise. Will catch the next flight out." There was a pause as she rose to her feet. She looked towards the door and then back at Patrick to deliver her final words. "I wish I could say it was good seeing you again but, well, you know. Thank you for trusting me with this. It means a lot; especially after everything I put you through, before. Take care of yourself."

With that, she was gone.

McGinty, Armchair Detective
Logan Bruce

McGinty rapped on the door, and waited for a response.

'I've been expecting you,' a voice said in a strong Transylvanian accent as the door slowly swung open. The occupant, a well-dressed man with perfectly combed hair, paused as he examined the newcomer. 'Meester ...'

'McGinty,' the detective replied in a broad Irish-American drawl. Almost matter-of-factly he put his hand on his hip, pushing his raincoat open to reveal a Baltimore Police badge on his hip. 'Detective McGinty.'

'Delighted to meet you. How may I be of assistance?'

'You are Doctor Hannibal Smith, I presume?'

'A Doctor of Psychiatry, if that is what you need.'

'I was passing through the neighbourhood, and I remembered your advert on the e-mail group,' McGinty sighed. 'You suggested other members might want to meet you here to to discuss some matters.'

'Concerning your alcoholism?' the shrink replied.

'No, that comes with the territory,' McGinty smirked. 'I have to drink hard as part of my job as a crime-solving detective. If I actually had a good home life, people would suspect that I was not selflessly sacrificing my own happiness to ensure their security. If that happened, they would lose confidence in the police. Anarchy would take hold. Think about it. All the best detectives are embittered loners, and we can only solve our toughest cases while we are on suspension from regular duty.'

The shrink considered this for a moment. 'Come in, then.'

McGinty followed his host into the living room, and took the seat that was indicated to him. The enormous widescreen television set was on, showing a police procedural show. The room was neat, tidy - almost too much so. In fact, it was immaculate, as if occupied by an obsessive-compulsive. But then, his own place was the opposite. Just because the bins had been emptied and there were no mystery stains on the carpet, was nothing in itself to be suspicious of.

McGinty looked at the shrink again, and sized him up. Yes, he was the kind of neat-freak who belonged in a place like this. Take the bins out? He probably even did his recycling regularly every week!

'If you don't mind me saying, there's something I've been wondering about,' McGinty said.

'Oh?' The shrink's tone was even, measured, unemotional.

'Your plaque outside reads Dr John Smith, but the e-mail said to ask for Hannibal.'

'How very observant,' the shrink replied dryly. 'You should be a Detective.'

'Hardy frigging har.'

'In answer to your question, Hannibal is my middle name. My full name is John Hannibal Smith. When I arrived in this country, my nickname was Hannibal the Colonel.'

'So Smith is not your real name?'

'A name is only something people call you. A rose by any other name would smell as sweet. We also considered using the surname Solo. My brother's name was Napoleon, so we could have built on the theme.'

'Well, can I call you Hannibal?'

'Please do ... Detective?'

'McGinty. Just McGinty. My friends call me McGinty, everyone else calls me DETECTIVE McGinty. It helps keep people straight.'

'I'll bet it does. Anyhow, back to work. I was just reviewing a couple of cases. Perhaps you could lend your own expertise.'

'Certainly,' McGinty said.

'Good. Would you like a snack? I've been told I cook the best bacon sandwiches in the city. That's what they say, anyway'

'I could do with some of that.' McGinty hadn't eaten in hours, so this offer of a free snack was much appreciated.

Hannibal disappeared into the kitchen area, leaving the door ajar for continued conversation.

'You're in luck,' Hannibal announced through the door. 'I have a couple of slices left.'

'Don't go to any trouble on my account,' McGinty replied, just to be polite. The aroma of sizzling bacon wafted through the open doorway, and he felt hungrier than ever.

'It's no trouble,' Hannibal said. 'I've been meaning to get rid of that batch, because I'm expecting to put some fresh pig meat in my freezer quite soon.'

'Glad to hear it.' But the only thing McGinty would be glad of was some actual food.

Hannibal emerged from the kitchen, a bottle of red wine in one hand and a pair of glasses in the other. He set them down on the coffee table, and took the armchair opposite McGinty.

'It'll be ready in a couple of minutes,' Hannibal announced as he started to unscrew the wine cork..

'There's some blood on your cuff.' McGinty pointed at Hannibal's right wrist. 'Did you nick yourself on the carving knife?'

'I'm sorry,' Hannibal replied in his heavy Eastern European accent. 'I split some claret earlier. While we are on the subject, would you like a glass of red wine?'

'Do you have any whiskey?'

'I have some Bushmills.'

'Bushmills?' McGinty was aghast at the suggestion. 'That's Protestant whiskey!'

'The blood of Christ compels you,' the shrink smiled. He poured two glasses of red wine, and handed one to McGinty.

'Slainte!' McGinty clinked his glass against Hannibal's, and took a sip. 'So, what are these cases you wish to discuss?'

'The first is that of the Chesapeake Cutter.'

'Well, to start with, that's a terrible name. He sounds like a Batman villain.'

'I hope you realise that professional detectives refer to a serial perpetrator as an UnSub, as in Unknown Subject. The fancy nicknames are usually foisted upon them by sleazy tabloid journalists.'

'I know that!' McGinty snapped. 'I was trying to lighten the mood.'

'This is a serious matter. Can we continue?'

'Certainly,' McGinty sighed. 'What is the Cutter's geographical range?'

'He's quite mobile, but the victims are all within the Greater Baltimore area.'

'All the ones you know of, that is.'

'Good point.' Hannibal almost seemed to smirk a little.

'Were the victims sexually assaulted?' McGinty asked.

'No.'

'Then the motive was the kill ... and the trophy.' McGinty

paused a second. 'What organs did he take?'

'Different ones every time. They could be for transplants - except for the intestines.'

'Tobias used his victims' entrails to make violin strings.'

'No, this was not Tobias' doing.' Hannibal seemed strangely insistent. 'The Cutter wanted the intestines for something else.'

'What can you make from intestines? A football? A belt?'

'No, the leather would not be strong enough. The only other suggestion anyone made was sausages.'

'Well, we can get back to that later.' McGinty glanced back at the kitchen, wondering where his bacon sandwich was. 'What else do we know about him?'

'The wounds of the victims indicate the Cutter extracted his medical trophies with surgical precision.'

'Medical knowledge such as basic human anatomy does not make him a doctor,' McGinty sighed. 'Amateur Ripperologists often assume that it does.'

'The Cutter didn't just cut the victims open and remove organs - he tied them off.'

'What? Like a professional surgeon?'

'That's right.'

'Did he use any particular technique?'

'The Medical Examiner says the method used was in standard practice across North America.'

'Then the Cutter attended Medical School in the USA or Canada.' McGinty knew how important this clue was, because only a tiny number of people had access to that level of education. 'More than that, he practiced as a surgeon. That has to narrow the field of suspects quite a bit. What else have we got to narrow the field?'

'Jack Crawford got some interesting feedback from his FBI trainee, Marion. She said she thought he was Caucasian, but exotic ...'

'Like an immigrant?'

'Yes. Maybe she meant Canadian, Australian, South African, Dutch ... East European, perhaps.'

'What did Marion say to you?'

'She disappeared a year ago. The Cutter caught her, locked her up and recorded her cries for help. Then he phoned Jack Crawford and played the tape, just to mess with him.'

'Why go to all that trouble?'

'He wanted to mess up the case, to throw Jack Crawford off track.'

'So why not just kill him?'

'If he's dead, they'll just replace him. But alive, he's a distraction.'

'So the Cutter wants Jack Crawford alive. But he knows Jack is too close.'

'He has a relationship with him.'

'He could just form a relationship with Jack's replacement.'

'No, not if his relationship is social.'

'So it's someone Jack Crawford socialised with, maybe had dinner with ...'

McGinty's stomach began to growl at the mention of dinner.

'It sounds like this Marion was really onto something. How did the Cutter get her?'

'She broke protocol and continued an investigation by herself. No backup, nothing. Real Dirty Harry stuff.'

'What a cliche,' McGinty sighed. 'Why do people on these shows always make the same stupid mistakes? Do they never watch TV?'

'It is called genre blindness,' Hannibal replied. 'Like in the zombie movies, they never use the word zombie. That is because they exist in a parallel universe where zombie movies do not exist, but actual zombies do.'

'So does that mean that because we have movies about serial killers, we can't have serial killers in real life?'

'No, that's just you being meta.'

'Oh. So what if the whole universe is fictional except for the man who is imagining it?'

'That is a form of philosophy known as solipsism.'

'Oh. So they didn't just invent it for the Matrix?'

'No.'

'There is something I've been wondering.'

'Oh yes?'

'The slasher movie. What genre is it? It can't be horror, because the classic slasher film lacks a supernatural aspect. So it must be crime, because the crime genre is horror minus the supernatural. But something about that just does not seem right to me.'

'You are quite right,' Hannibal smiled. 'The slasher sub-genre, as it has evolved from the classic Italian Giallo format, shares aspects of both horror and crime genres. In fact, it is a true cross-genre format. This is easier to understand if one regards the slasher as being a horror-dunnit, a term which adequately sums up its mixed genre roots.'

'So what Genre is Lord Of The Rings?'

'Fantasy Adventure, of course.'

'Ah! But there is magic in it. So is it not horror too?'

'No, think of the setting. If Frodo had stayed home and been chased round the Shire by the Horsemen and Gollum, it would be horror. But Frodo was an active protagonist who went on the Hero's Quest. By definition it's action adventure.'

'So, What about Detective Fiction? Detectives are active protagonists.'

'No they aren't. They react, they can only investigate after the crime has been committed. And if a murder has supernatural origins, it's a horror genre story.'

'Speaking of slasher killers, how many victims has the Cutter claimed lately?'

'Lately, none.' Hannibal put down his glass, and folded his fingers neatly together. 'The Cutter's last recorded kill was Marion herself, over a year ago.'

'Maybe he is dead.'

'He came up for air when he thought someone was copycatting him. He was still alive when he left Marion's severed arm for Bill to find, a couple of weeks ago.'

'You mentioned copycatting. That makes me think. Did they ever catch the guy who copycatted the Minnesota Shrike?'

'No, not yet. You think ...'

'We're looking for the Shrike's copycat, and the Cutter is looking for someone to copy. Perhaps ...'

'Perhaps ...?'

'Perhaps he is copycatting ... disguising his kills as the work of his rivals.'

'He helps the police take them out, leaving more victims for him.'

'Like Dexter, you mean?'

'I never watched that show. It all seemed a bit far-fetched.'

'You mean the idea that a serial killer could help detectives investigating murders?'

'No, it's the actual number of serial killers he just happens to bump into in his tiny city. The FBI estimates there are only thirty active serial killers in the USA at any one time. That's one in ten million people.'

'So what? Baltimore isn't that big, but still has an average of about one murder a day.'

'Think of it this way. Baltimore has a population of what, a million people?'

'In the greater Baltimore area, perhaps.'

'Okay. So what is the population of Cabot Cove?'

'A thousand times less.'

'But is the body count a thousand times less?'

'Are you implying that Mrs Marbles is the killer? Possibly the most successful serial killer ever?'

'Hey, if it's true in Dexter, it can be true in any show.'

'That's why I never believe those TV shows. They just pay no attention to realism. There is at least one serial killer every single week, so they deal with dozens every year. The cops in the show always solve their case within 42 minutes, plus commercial breaks. It's just unbelievable. I mean, they get DNA results back in five minutes while in real life the Vegas crime lab had a one-year backlog.'

'And what about the Behavioural Science detectives?'

'Their computerised record searches - instantaneous technology with no warrants required - it's a complete fiction, to allow the writers to tie up the story within 42 minutes. But because of these damn shows, peoples' expectations when it comes to their daily interaction with law enforcement are unrealistically high. In real life it takes YEARS to catch a serial killer.'

'Like the Cutter. He's gone dormant, or more likely he's disguising his kills by copycatting other killers. But if he broke cover when someone copycatted him ...'

McGinty paused for a moment.

'How did he preserve Marion's arm? Does he have knowledge of taxidermy or embalming?'

'No, it was frozen.'

'That made me think of something,' McGinty said. 'Do you serve any ice with your whiskey?'

'In the freezer,' Dr Smith said. 'Don't bother yourself, I'll go get it.'

'The freezer .. with the meat.' McGinty glanced back at the kitchen. 'That's why he froze Marion's arm, and the other organs he stole. He keeps them as meat. He's eating them!'

'What a terrible thought.' Hannibal's face was as placid as ever. 'But on the bright side, your bacon sandwich should be ready by now.'

I hope it was worth the wait, McGinty thought as Hannibal disappeared into the kitchen.

The shrink returned with a tray containing a couple of plates, each with a beautifully cooked bacon and cheese sandwich.

'Eat up,' Hannibal said as he offered one to McGinty.

McGinty eagerly accepted, and bit deep into the sweet-tasting meaty snack.

'They say the bacon sandwich was invented so some Englishman could play cards and eat lunch at the same time.'

'Ah yes, the Earl of Sandwich. The story goes that back then the cuts of meat they had were very fatty, and he used the bread as a moisture barrier to keep his fingers dry. Nobody wants to leave nasty greasy fingerprints all over the place, do they now?'

McGinty glanced at his fingers, took the hint and wiped them carefully on his napkin.

'Sorry,' he said as he caught his host's eye.'

'So, who do you think the Chesapeake Cutter is?' Hannibal asked.

'It could be anyone,' McGinty shrugged. 'Hey, didn't you say there were TWO cases you were interested in?'

'The other one is the Baltimore person who has been biting homeless people,' Hannibal said.

McGinty tried not to choke on his sandwich, and avoided Hannibal's laser stare.

'My profile on the Baltimore Biter is simple,' Hannibal announced. 'The killer is a Caucasian male, middle class, possibly a Government employee, hates his job, passed over for promotion ...'

'Could be anyone,' McGinty shrugged.

'Not in a Black working-class city like Baltimore,' the Doctor smirked.

'Is that all?'

'He is a high-functioning alcoholic, possibly with homosexual tendencies.'

'Could be ...' McGinty shrugged, 'a lot of people. Keep going.'

'The bites are post-mortem, indicating staging. Such a ritual is itself indicative of a knowledge of police procedure. The lack of other forensic evidence indicates a high forensic awareness.'

'He probably watched a lot of those police procedural TV shows,' McGinty replied.

'No, as we both know they are notoriously inaccurate and sacrifice realism for dramatic effect. I suspect this killer learned police procedure the hard way, through employment in law enforcement.'

'A cop,' McGinty hissed.

'Possibly,' the shrink replied.

McGinty turned to face him, and felt the man's piercing blue eyes cut right through him. 'I think I know who the most logical suspect is,' McGinty smirked.

'Really?'

'Yes, we have a winner! I'd love to get a team ready for the take-down. He's our man. I know, it couldn't happen to a nicer guy.'

'So what's your course of action?'

'I'd take out my cell-phone and hit the speed-dial for the sergeant who had run the surveillance detail. Then tell him to get the tapes of that gay bar he ran a stakeout on last year. Take a look through them. There is someone he'll recognise - not socially, it's someone from the Department!'

McGinty's smirk expanded into a wide grin.

'There is clear evidence against the Baltimore Biter. The DA should draw up an arrest warrant for Deputy Chief Rawls. They've got him on means, motive and opportunity.'

'You are preaching to the converted,' Hannibal assured him. 'Couldn't you just shout at the television like normal people?'

'Ok,' McGinty sighed, and turned to the television set. 'Hey you, it's him! He's the serial killer! How can you not see it?'

The characters on the television show continued on their pre-scripted dialogues, ignoring all suggestions from the audience in the living room.

'Okay, I'm bored with this,' McGinty said. 'What other shows have you been watching lately?'

In the Closet?
Logan Bruce

McGinty awoke on a couch. Not his own couch, he realised as he gazed around the room. He hadn't made it back from the party, it seemed. Along with half the other guests, he had been allowed to crash for the night in the hostess's living room.

He staggered down the corridor to the hostess's room, then rapped on the door and waited for a response.

'What's up?' a voice asked from behind him.

McGinty turned, and found himself face to face with Javier the house-boy.

'Where's Alice?' McGinty asked.

'It's in Australia?' the hired help replied, perplexed. 'Where it always is.'

'No, I mean Alice Smyth.' McGinty decided to dumb things down for the poor man's benefit. 'Not the town of Alice bloody Springs. I mean Mrs Smyth, the woman who lives here!'

'She's in her room. She was taking her diamond back to the walk-in closet.'

'How long ago as that?'

'It was -' Javier looked at his watch. 'That can't be right! It's morning already.'

'When did she go in?'

'It was just a couple of minutes ago. Seemed like it was, that is. 4AM, I think.'

'And she hasn't come out past you this whole time?'

'No - why?'

'She was meant to meet me - but she must still be in the closet.'

McGinty knocked on the door again. 'Alice, are you in there?' Still there was no answer.

'Maybe she got drunk and passed out,' Javier suggested.

'Was she drinking the last time you saw her?'

'Well, no ...'

'Does she have a huge stack of booze in her closet?'

'Not that I know of, but I haven't been in there.'

McGinty twisted the door-handle, but the door refused to

budge.

'Locked from the inside,' he said aloud. 'She hasn't come out of the room, and she's not responding to loud knocking. She can't just be asleep - she would have woken up by now. She's either unconscious, comatose or dead. We'd better break this door down ASAP!'

'What on earth do you think you're doing?' a shrill voice shrieked from behind them.

They spun round, expecting to see Alice somehow behind them.

It was Lena the house-maid, her foul mood probably due to the realization that she was the one who was going to have top clean up the entire house after the previous night's barbecue and booze-up.

The two men looked at each other.

'It's Alice,' McGinty ventured. 'She's locked herself in her room and now she won't answer the door. She's unconscious - or worse. Maybe passed out in a puddle of her own sick. We need to break the door down -'

Lena held her keyring aloft. 'We could just unlock the door like civilised people. Or is that too much thinking for you brain-boxes?'

McGinty and Javier stepped aside, and let Lena do the necessary. The door swung inwards.

'Oh my god -' Lena gasped, and the two men pushed past her into the bedroom.

The bed was pristine; it had not been slept in. The whole room was immaculate, but there was no sign of Alice.

'She's not here,' McGinty began.

'The Closet!' Javier hissed, and stepped towards the side wall. The bookcase pushed easily aside, and behind it was a closet the size of some peoples' bedrooms. The left wall was dresses - sparkly, shiny, no two alike. The right hand wall was shoes - racks and racks of shoes, each pair perfectly selected to match one of the fancy dresses on the opposing wall. On the far wall was a solid-looking display case containing the most exquisite and imaginative jewelery imaginable. Right in the centre was a massive diamond pendant - the one McGinty had seen Alice wearing the night before.

'So she put the diamond pendant back,' McGinty said aloud. 'Just like you said. But where is she now?'

Javier shrugged, mystified. 'All I know is, she had the pendant, and she took it to her room to put it back in the closet. And now ...'

'If she didn't leave by the door,' McGinty mused, 'maybe she slipped out a window.'

McGinty strode out of the closet, and went straight to the window beside the bed. The frame did not budge when he gave it a tug - there was a small keyhole lined with black rubber for waterproofing, he realised. Goddamn double-glazing, he thought, those things are never to open even under the best of circumstances. They'll be a goddamn nightmare in a fire evacuation, that's for sure. But since the windows were apparently locked from the inside. As was the door, there was no way Alice could have gotten out.

'Okay, so were is she?' McGinty asked the other two. He knelt by the bed, pulled the sheets up, and peered underneath.

Nothing.

Lena had done a great job of keeping the place clean, he had to admit. He would like to have her around at his place a few times a week - he glimpsed her ever-scowling face, and thought the better of making the suggestion to her. The poor girl always had a chip on her shoulder; she always thought that better-educated people were looking down their noses at her.

A thought suddenly occurred to McGinty. 'We'll have to wake Hannibal and the others and let them know. Maybe they saw or heard something.'

'That lot?' Javier scoffed. 'They all passed out drunk by 3AM. They've been sleeping it off on the air-mattresses. They won't be fit for anything until after brunch.'

'Brunch ...' Lena said.

McGinty caught her expression - mournful, as if she had suddenly stopped blaming the universe for all of her problems.

'What is it?' McGinty asked.

She met his eye, and instead of snapping his head off and telling him not to cross-examine her she said 'Alice told me not to bother about Brunch. I thought it was odd - it's her favourite meal of the day. I think she knew something would happen to her - something bad.'

'Did she seem depressed?'

'No! No ...'

'But she could have been covering for something?'
Lena did not answer.
'Has anything bad happened to her lately?'
'She broke up with her boyfriend. I never thought he was right for her, they didn't seem to be a great couple, and I thought she'd finally realised it herself. She seemed to be okay with the break-up.'
'But she could have been hiding something deeper?'
'Not from me she couldn't.' Lena was adamant.
McGinty held his own opinion. If Alice knew something bad was going to happen, and did nothing to save herself, then she must have committed herself to her fate. Even if she wasn't directly responsible for it herself.
What do you think happened to her,' he asked Lena.
She pointed accusingly. 'Javier was the last one to see her alive!'
'You are assuming she is no longer alive,' Javier pleaded.
'The chances are that she is dead,' McGinty announced, 'and her body is concealed somewhere in the room. Like the woman stuffed up the chimney in "Murders in the Rue Morgue". In fact, there are rules for locked room mysteries.'
'What do you mean?'
'Back in the twenties or thirties, when detective fiction was all the craze, a writer sat down and wrote out the ten different types of solution to locked room mysteries. Every possible solution to the locked room problem is a spin on one of those ten.'
'So what are they?'
'Well, I don't know. Not offhand, anyway. Hell, most people don't even know they exist. But they're on the internet. We can do a web search for them.'
McGinty pulled out his smart-phone, and switched it on.
The "Battery too low" warning flashed up.
'Damn. Has anyone got a charger?'
'No need.' Javier held his own phone aloft. 'I've got battery ... but no signal.'
'Seriously? Talk about cliches!'
'These damn phones. We rely on them for everything, but they never work when you really need them.'
'We could use it to call the cops.'

'No need,' McGinty snarled. 'I'm a detective, remember?'

'Uh ...' Javier and Lena looked at each other. 'Yeah ...'

'You talk all this detective talk,' Lena glared accusingly at McGinty. 'But what crimes have you ever solved? Real crimes, not just ones in TV shows?'

'I can solve this,' McGinty assured her.

'How do we know that you didn't do this yourself?' Javier asked. 'You could cause the crime, then pretend to solve it so you can be a big hero. Like firemen who light fires so they can put it out.'

'Well, I can name an actual suspect and I have actual physical evidence to prove what I say,' McGinty said.

'Okay, hotshot. What is this evidence?'

'Lena had the only key to the bedroom.'

All eyes swiveled to Lena.

'It's not the only key.'

'Really? Then why was the other key not in the keyhole on the other side?'

'Well, how can you be certain that it wasn't?'

'Because if there was a key on the inside of the keyhole, it would have been impossible for you to fit your key in from the outside. But your key fitted perfectly, hence there was no other key.'

'You ...' Lena was speechless. 'Son of a -'

'Brunch?' A distinctive tone cut through the argument. 'Did someone say Brunch?'

McGinty looked round, and saw Hannibal standing in the doorway. His usually pristine haircut was unkempt and bedraggled.

'It was wishful thinking,' McGinty replied. 'And you look as hung over as hell. You should go back to the air mattress and sleep it off.'

'You look just like I feel,' Javier interjected, but Hannibal just ignored him.

'I need a glass of milk to settle my stomach,' Hannibal grumbled as he stumbled past the others into the kitchen.

'Hey, Hannibal,' McGinty called. 'When you're breaking in the new kitchen, can you whip us up some bacon butties?'

Hannibal did not look back at him, merely raised a hand with a single impudent digit on display.

'McGinty, what is this strange fixation you have with food?' Lena asked.

'I eat when I'm nervous.'
'You're always eating. Are you always nervous?'
'I also eat when I'm hungry. Which is a lot of the time.'
'I was going to say it was a sign of a guilty conscience.'
'What can I say, I like the finer things in life. I'm a gourmet. Food is my substitute for sex, so I eat five meals a day.'
'Are you flirting with me?' Lena asked. 'Because if you are, I have to tell you that you are not very good at it.'
'Are you trying to distract me?' McGinty replied. 'Because as I recall, you are still our main suspect in Alice's disappearance.'
'You cannot be serious!'
'Well, I am deadly serious. The lady of the house is gone, and the housekeeper and manservant are both messing me about.'
'Housekeeper?' Lena gasped.
'Manservant?' Javier snorted.
'Yes, I know Alice is too proud to call you that, but I cannot deny the truth any longer. The big cliché of classic detective stories is that the butler did it. And since you two are the nearest thing to a butler ...'
'A couple of things,' Lena interjected. 'Firstly, this is not the Nineteen Thirties. Nobody has servants any more.'
'Alice evidently does, or you two would not be here.'
'We are not her servants,' Javier hissed. 'We are her flat-mates.'
'Oh.' McGinty started to think he may have missed a major piece of information. 'So you both have day jobs, and pay money towards your share of the rent?'
'Well, no,' Lena replied.
'We cut a deal with Alice,' Javier said. 'We keep the place tidy for her, and she covers the rent and the grocery shopping bills.'
'So you do domestic chores in exchange for free food and a place to live,' McGinty asked.
'That's right,' Javier said.
'It's not what it sounds like,' Lena replied.
'Oh, I get the feeling it's EXACTLY what it sounds like,' McGinty smirked. 'You aren't actual servants, you just do the work of servants and get the pay of servants in exchange.'
'Well, technically ...'
'Thank you for explaining it to me,' McGinty said. 'Now, did

you have another point to make?'

'Actually, I did,' Lena said. 'Firstly, Javier and I have the most to lose if anything happens to Alice, because she is our meal ticket.'

'That makes sense,' McGinty agreed. 'Anything else you have to say?'

My secondary point is this. You talked about the nineteen thirties classic detective story cliché that the butler did it. But the modern cliche is that the detective investigating a case is also the crook at the heart of the case. It is a despicable cliché, but it still abounds.'

'You can't blame it on me,' McGinty said.

'What do you mean?' Lena asked. 'The violence or the cliché?'

'Both, I suppose.'

'Hey, everyone,' a familiar voice called from the front door.

They turned as one, and gasped in shock at what they saw.

'Alice?' McGinty mouthed. 'What the hell are you doing there?'

Alice stepped aside, and a girl in a bakery apron stepped past her with a tray of freshly-baked croissants.

'You know me,' Alice smiled. 'I'm an early riser. While you lot were sleeping, I nipped out to get everyone some Brunch!'

"Who Burned Billizabeth?"
The antidote to locked-room mysteries
Logan Bruce

McGinty rapped on the door, and waited for a response.

'So what are we watching today?" McGinty asked as Hannibal opened the front door. 'Crime and Order, or illegal intent? Not that it matters, all these Detective shows tend to blur together these days'

'Haven't you heard?' Hannibal asked, as he opened the door wider and let McGinty walk in. 'Television has been cancelled for tonight.'

'What? All channels, you mean?'

'Yes, I'm afraid so.'

'How the hell can that happen? Has there been another 9-11? Or someone like Princess Diana died in spectacular circumstances?'

'Worse.' Hannibal paused, as if for dramatic effect. 'Someone burned Billizabeth.'

'What?'

'You heard me. Someone burned Billizabeth.'

'You know, I have absolutely no idea what any of that actually means. '

'Are you serious?' For the first time McGinty could remember, Hannibal's rigid face showed an expression of surprise. 'You don't know about William and Elizabeth?'

'Are they a Royal couple?'

'No! Quite the opposite - they are Hollywood Royalty, a pair of bona fide celebrities.'

'You'll forgive me if I use the term oxymoron,' McGinty replied dryly. 'In my experience, a celebrity is a talentless nobody who is famous because they are in the public eye, not because they made an actual achievement. And what idiot came up with the idea of calling them Billizabeth?'

'It comes from the idea of creating a hybrid name from the names of the two persons who constitute the couple. First there was Bennifer, then Brangelina. Today the newest, hottest celebrity couple, Billizabeth, were about to get married. But their top-security wedding was gatecrashed ... webcast to the entire Internet.'

'Well, that must be a burn, in the That 70s Show sense.'

'Not that kind of burn,' Hannibal replied as he lifted his remote control and thumbed a button. The television hummed to life.

'I told you the Press managed to sneak in a web-cam,' Hannibal said as he turned the sound down and flicked through the channels. He stopped on one as a news broadcast came on air.

Despite the web-cam footage's pixelation, exaggerated by the wide-screen TV's high definition, McGinty could make out the interior of a church. A man in a tuxedo stood alone at the front, with his back to the camera.

'It's badly positioned,' McGinty noted. 'You can't see his face.'

'But you can make out that he has a bad toupee,' Hannibal replied.

McGinty squinted. 'You're right,' he conceded. 'I hope that's not the highlight of this show.'

A woman in a white dress and veil walked into shot, and joined the tuxedo man in the centre of the screen. From the darkness behind them, a white-collared churchman hovered into view.

Suddenly, a flicker of flame appeared over the tuxedo man's right shoulder. In a second, the flame had spread to engulf his entire torso. The woman turned to run, but her bridal dress must have brushed against him because before she could take a step she was on fire herself.

'What the hell happened?' McGinty asked.

The web-cam footage was replaced on the screen with head-shot photos of a man and woman that McGinty recognised from the front cover of tabloid newspapers.

'That is world history in the making,' Hannibal announced. 'Billizabeth was not just a pair of celebrities, they were a movie star couple - and this public death scene has turned them from the new Brangelina into the new JFK and Marilyn Monroe.'

'But what caused the fire?'

'As far as they can tell, it was Spontaneous Human Combustion. The bodies were entirely carbonized, with no DNA left.'

'Was it a bomb?'

'You may as well suggest magic, or maybe Bill was a vampire who got caught in sunlight. Or someone used a microwave weapon mounted on an overflying plane or satellite.'

'You are not being constructive,' McGinty snarled. 'My curiosity will not be satiated until we get an explanation. A plausible one, at least.'

'Let me tell you a story,' Hannibal said. 'It is about the most famous man in the world. A man so well-known that decades later his name and face were iconic throughout the world. He was the leader of the greatest superpower the world had ever known at that time. And yet he was murdered in broad daylight in the middle of a street in a major city in his own country. This happened in front of a massive crowd of onlookers, it was photographed and filmed, and the evidence has been freely and publicly available for decades afterward.'

'Bull-' McGinty interrupted.

'Let me finish,' Hannibal said. He lifted a paperback copy of Robert Heinlein's "Friday", flicked through it, and read aloud.

'Killed in front of hundreds of witnesses and every aspect, before, during and after, heavily documented. All that mountain of evidence adds up to is this: nobody knows who shot him, how many shot him, how many times he was shot, who did it, why it was done, and who was involved in the conspiracy, if there was a conspiracy. It isn't even possible to say whether the murder plot was foreign or domestic ... if it is impossible to untangle one that recent and that thoroughly investigated, what chance is there of figuring out the details of the conspiracy that did in Gaius Iulius Caesar? Or Guy Fawkes and the Gunpowder plot? All that can truthfully be said is that the people who come out on top write the official versions found in the history books, history that is no more honest than autobiography.'

'But that was a long time ago,' McGinty said. 'Technology has come forward a long way since the Zapruder film. Modern Hollywood is a goldfish bowl more than ever now.'

'There has been FBI surveillance on Hollywood names for decades,' Hannibal told him. 'Hoover's pre-emptive surveillance policy was called CoIntelPro, and it included getting blackmail material on anyone who might fall foul of Joe McCarthy. I have no doubt that it was revived after 9/11, to target all the anti-war, anti-gun and anti-oil types lurking among Hollywood's perceived Liberal intelligentsia.'

'I'm a detective,' McGinty snarled. 'I know all about CoIntelPro. But I wasn't talking about Big Brother. I meant Little Brother - the average citizens who have home video cameras, like the guy who videotaped the Rodney King beating.'

'You mean the people who will use their phone to video a crime and post it on the Internet rather than just use the phone to call the police?'

'Yes, that's exactly what I mean,' McGinty said.

'That is the thin end,' Hannibal said. 'Ever since 9-11 the Government has given itself more surveillance powers, and invested more money in using those powers.'

'There is a moral to this,' McGinty said. 'You can video some of the people all of the time, and all of the people some of the time. But Big Government will ultimately attempt to video all the people all of the time.'

'Bastards!' Hannibal spat. 'But there is one major fact in evidence. In this day and age, in the modern high-tech surveillance society, every mystery is a locked room mystery.'

'So what?'

'This could be the case of the century!' Hannibal pointed enthusiastically at the television set, which was re-showing the web-cam footage on a loop.

'That's a bit premature,' McGinty said.

'How so?'

'Well, to start with the century isn't even a quarter of the way through yet. Also, it hasn't been established yet that any actual crime was committed.'

'That is why I said CASE of the century instead of CRIME of the century.'

'Nice distinction. But it's not a case unless we are private detectives paid to investigate the incident. Which, I should remind you, we are not.'

'You are a professional police detective,' Hannibal reminded him.

McGinty hesitated, as if considering how best to reply. 'My status as a police officer is irrelevant. This incident happened outside my jurisdiction, so I cannot legally investigate it.'

'Perhaps not. But you can join me on a trip to Holywood. I've made all the arrangements.'

'Fine by me,' McGinty said. 'After all, there will be nothing decent on television tonight.'

McGinty followed Hannibal to the car, and got in the

passenger seat. The shrink was a solid driver, and their journey through the city centre was uneventful.

McGinty saw the sign for the George Best airport coming up, and realised something.

'I don't have my passport,' he said.

'You won't need it,' Hannibal said as he drove past the Airport entrance and continued along the road to Bangor. 'This is a road trip.'

'A road trip? To Hollywood, California? Wouldn't that be a plane trip'

'It would be, but that is not the Holywood I have in mind.'

McGinty felt the enthusiasm flow out of him as Hannibal followed the road signs towards Holywood, County Down. After all, what if he had been offered the chance to go to New York City, and instead ended up in old York?

'So what did you think of the ending to Breaking Bad?' Hannibal asked, evidently perturbed by McGinty's sullen silence..

'I've never watched it.'

'They say that it's the new The Wire.'

'That's what they say. But I don't care if it's the new Sopranos or Shield. But I wouldn't watch them either. I don't want to watch any show that glamourises crime.'

'Really? So what about shows that have a cop bending the rules or going undercover, making friends with crooks? Or what about a show where a serial killer helps to catch other killers?'

'Well, that's different.'

'How so?'

'A crooked cop isn't really a villain; he's just a normal guy in a tough situation.'

'Normal? You think it's normal to fall prey to temptation, to get corrupted by power, and take the easy way out?'

'Stealing from crooks is a victimless crime. Everyone knows that.'

'By that logic, so is shoplifting or punching someone when the lights are out.'

'Don't you quote the Simpsons at me!'

'So you're not denying the truth?'

'To hell with you!'

'You are a sore loser in debates, McGinty.'

'Hey, is this place we're looking for anywhere near here, or will we be driving about all night?'

'It's on this street,' Hannibal said as he pulled the car over to the side of the road. 'In fact, we just passed it.'

'And you think they have what we want?' McGinty hissed as he opened the car door.

'There is only one way to find out. But we must employ subtlety and caution on this mission. Like a pair of spies,' he added.

'You know what this is like?' McGinty found himself almost giddy with excitement over the important and dangerous mission. Despite what he told people, he did not do as much field work as he wanted them to believe. 'It's like one of those CIA versus KGB stories - like a retro 1960s James Bond story.'

'Really?'

'Yes, really. Don't you agree?'

'Yes, I agree. I'm just surprised that you don't seem to know the term The ... Cold ... War.'

'There's a term for it?' McGinty laid on the sarcasm, but Hannibal just seemed to ignore it.

'Yes, there is indeed a term.'

'So what's the plan?' McGinty tried to change the subject. 'How are we going to bluff our way in?'

'We will pose as Gideons.'

'Who or what are Gideons?'

'Gideons are a Christian sect who hand out Bibles. You know all the bibles in hotel rooms? Those are Gideon bibles, put there by Gideons. So we will pose as Gideons.'

'Are the Gideons like the book fairies?' McGinty joked. 'Do they creep in at midnight and stick a book under your pillow?'

Hannibal fixed him with a murderous gaze.

They stopped outside a big white house with a perfectly manicured front lawn. McGinty looked it over. The Guest House sign on the front lawn said "Bateman Bed & Breakfast", while the front window had a note saying "Help wanted: Experience Essential".

Hannibal rang the doorbell.

The front door opened, and a pleasant-faced gentleman appeared. He smiled broadly, a little too widely for McGinty's comfort. He was clean-shaven, of indeterminate age, and somehow reminded McGinty of Cliff Richard.

'Good evening,' the man said. 'I'm the proprietor. Call me Norm.'

'Pleased to meet you,' McGinty said.

'Would you like a room each ... or a double room, perhaps?'

'Actually, we're not here for a room,' Hannibal said.

'Are you gentlemen here about the job? We need someone to help out. We've been short-staffed ever since Aunt Alice left us.'

'Whatever happened to Aunt Alice?' McGinty asked.

'That's a good film,' Hannibal interjected. 'I thought of getting a housekeeper after I saw it.'

'I assumed your place was spotless because you are ...'

'Fastidious?' Hannibal offered.

'Not a word I would normally use, but it carries the meaning. Anyway, it never occurred to me that you cheated and hired a housekeeper to keep the place tidy.'

'Oh, I don't have a housekeeper,' Hannibal said nonchalantly. 'Not any more, at least.'

'Actually, I'm looking to hire a housekeeper,' Norm said. 'I could really do with someone to lend a hand around here. I've got my hands full, I really do.'

'I'm afraid I am not much of a housekeeper,' Hannibal shrugged. 'But I am a gourmet chef. I minored in the culinary arts while an undergraduate, and I have kept myself handy with the knife ever since.'

'We could certainly do with a trained chef,' Norm beamed. 'Home cooking is all well and good, but I'm always short-staffed. If we had a professional like yourself here to help out ...'

'I can be available for early evening meals,' Hannibal said.

'We're glad to have you aboard.' Norm offered his hand, and Hannibal shook it.

'We?' McGinty queried. 'You keep saying "we" ...'

'My mother and I,' Norman replied.

'Is she ...' McGinty raised his eyes upwards, to indicate the heavens. 'Up there?'

Norm was aghast. 'You can't believe that I'm like some character in a gothic novel, keeping a vulnerable relative locked in the attic. No, mother's not here. She went away.'

'I'm sorry to hear that,' McGinty replied. 'My condolences.'

'Don't worry,' Norm smiled. 'She still talks to me. Tells me what to do, you know. She's still running the old place in spirit, you know?'

McGinty and Hannibal shared a glance.

Norm reached into his pocket.

McGinty moved his right foot back, into fighting poise, as his right hand came up ...

Norm's hand came up - holding a cell-phone.

'She calls me every day,' Norm said.

McGinty relaxed.

'It's good to talk,' Hannibal said, in his typical reassuring way. 'Now, how much does my new job pay?'

'Minimum wage, I'm afraid. Six pounds twenty an hour, two hours a day, seven days a week. Well, the good news is that it is less than fifteen hours a week, so it will not interfere with any benefits you are on. The bad news, it's only -'

'Eighty-six pounds and eighty pence a week,' Hannibal replied.

'If you do a good job we can push it up a bit,' Norm offered. 'I like nice round figures.'

'Shall I get started now?' Hannibal asked. 'It will be dinner time before we know it, and I want to familiarise myself with your kitchen before I get started.'

'Of course.' Norm ushered him in.

McGinty stepped up to follow.

'What about your friend?' Norm asked Hannibal.

'He is a Gideon,' Hannibal said. 'You can let him in, he is harmless.'

Norm stepped aside, and let McGinty in.

'I love handing out bibles,' McGinty said as he followed Hannibal down the hallway. 'They call me Bible John.'

'So where is your bible?' Norm asked.

'I've given them all out.'

'Shouldn't you be going back to get more?'

'Not at this time of day. The place will be closed by the time I get there.'

Down the corridor a toilet flushed, and they all turned to look at the source of the noise. The bathroom door opened, and a man stepped out clutching a hardback copy of "Modesty Blaise".

It took McGinty a moment to recognise him from the head-shot on the news broadcast.

Bill was older than he looked in the movies, with a touch of gray evident at his temples. He must have a special makeup assistant whose job it was to de-age him, McGinty thought. It could be worse. He could be like Sam Malone in the final season of Cheers, using vanity about his hair to hide the guilty secret of a toupee.

Their eyes locked, and Bill must have seen the expression of recognition on McGinty's face. He froze in horror.

It was Hannibal who broke the silence.

'Aren't you going to wash your hands?' the shrink asked.

'No need,' Bill shrugged. 'I had a shower earlier.'

'I don't quite see how that's relevant.'

'My cock is clean, and I didn't piss on my hands.'

'So you don't know about backsplash, then?'

'Backsplash?'

'Backsplash. It is when a liquid hits something, and splashes back towards its source.'

'Listen, I don't need to wash my hands!' Bill insisted.

'Then you'll forgive me if I don't shake hands with you.'

'That's fine by me.'

'What's all the commotion about?' a woman called from one of the rooms. A door opened, and she stepped out into the corridor ...

Elizabeth looked even worse than Bill. The flawless bone structure was there, of course, and rendered her instantly recognisable even though she had darkened her hair to its original shade. But what really made her look different was her skin - rough and uneven without the movie makeup troweled on.

'Perhaps you two should explain yourselves,' Hannibal said, a subtle edge to his voice that implied unpleasant consequences if they refused.

'I just couldn't handle the stress of being a celebrity any more,' Elizabeth pleaded. 'Our Wedding Planner was a former Secret Service agent who had guarded the President. She arranged decoy limos so the paparazzi couldn't follow us because they wouldn't know which one we were in. There was a closed list of guests and they were only to be sent hand-delivered invitations at the last minute. It was ridiculous the lengths we had to go to for a private ceremony. Then I realised the Wedding Dress had a veil, so nobody would realise if I had swapped places with my sister. She acts as my body double in movies sometimes. While the decoys distracted the Paparazzi, we could make our Honeymoon getaway. Once we take our make-up off, we look like average people - the fans do not recognise us.'

'So the fire was deliberate?' McGinty asked. 'The two people were stunt doubles, were they? Trained professionals?'

'No, it wasn't part of the plan. But I prefer to look on the bright side. Now we can retire, and live incognito with no stress. We can be the first Hollywood couple to actually have a happy marriage.'

While your sister and the fake Bill are crispy critters on a slab somewhere, McGinty thought. She was a completely narcissistic bitch, but was she also a murderer?

'So you could live out your lives incognito in a suburb of Belfast?' Hannibal evidently didn't think much of the plan either.

'Of course not,' Bill said. 'This is just a stop-off for us. Elizabeth is a major donor to a mine-clearing charity in certain Third World countries. The plan was to live in a luxury villa in a minefield in somewhere like Namibia or Cambodia.'

'If you find the creature comforts of County Down insufficient, you will not enjoy life in a Third World country,' Hannibal told him.

'Please, for God's sake,' Elizabeth begged. 'We've made it out of the rat-race. We have some privacy at last. Don't send us back into that goddamn goldfish bowl.'

Or to justice, McGinty thought, for the deaths of the two doubles who burned in the church.

'Of course not,' Hannibal smiled that crocodile smile of his. 'It would be a breach of my professional ethics.'

'Thanks,' Bill sighed.

'Ethics?' Elizabeth queried. She was obviously the brains of the two, McGinty realised.

'Yes, professional confidentiality. After all, I am a professional psychiatrist and you are both my patients.'

'We don't -' Bill began, but Elizabeth tapped him on the arm and he shushed. She had him well-trained, McGinty thought to himself.

'We'll pay whatever you want,' Elizabeth said.

'Excellent!'

'What about him?' Elizabeth pointed at McGinty.

'Don't worry about McGinty,' Hannibal smiled. 'My oath

covers him, because he is here in his professional capacity as my trusty manservant.'

'Manservant?' McGinty queried.

'It's a very well-paid position,' Hannibal replied, and nodded his head slightly towards Billizabeth.

McGinty took the hint. 'Aye, aye, Captain!'

'One last thing,' Hannibal said. 'If the fire was not deliberate, how did it start?'

'I hired a temporary stand-in at the last minute,' Bill said. 'The only one I could find with the same build was an alcoholic homeless man. He smelled like a distillery – he must have spilled some brandy or Poteen on himself, and it acted like an accelerant when exposed to a source of accidental ignition. Possibly from an electrical spark caused by a faulty microphone in the church.'

'A plausible explanation,' Hannibal declared. 'Come, McGinty – to the car.'

'But aren't you going to cook dinner?' Norm asked.

'Maybe some day,' Hannibal said. 'But I don't need the money any more, I've had a better offer.'

Hannibal strode out, and McGinty followed him again.

'There is one last mystery left to solve,' McGinty said as he got into the car. 'How on Earth did you know they would be here?'

'A few years ago I was in the Castlecourt shopping centre, looking to get a new pair of shoes, and I noticed a couple of tall blonde women nearby. One of them looked just like the actress from that TV show I liked so much, and the other was presumably her sister. And the irony is, a couple of years later she was interviewed in conjunction with her new film ... and she mentioned she had visited Belfast a few years previously. It wasn't a look-alike I saw, it was her! I could have said hello to her, but I didn't bother.'

'But how did you ... unless ... If that is the only time you saw her, then how did you know to look here?'

'Well ...' Hannibal hesitated. For the first time since he had met him, McGinty realised the shrink didn't have a comeback lined up.

'If she knew about the place to book it, and you knew that she knew ...' McGinty felt everything click into place. 'She was staying here back then, wasn't she?'

'Yes, that's right.' Hannibal was strangely quiet.

'But if you knew about this, that means that back then ...'

'You don't need to say it out loud.' Hannibal's voice was barely a whisper.

'You followed her here!'

'I said you didn't need to say it out loud.'

'Aye, aye, Captain!'

'I believe that cigars are in order,' Hannibal said as he opened the glove-box and reached inside. 'I love it when happenstance makes me seem clever!'

"Skeletons In The Closet"

TITANIA: Top Independent Talented Artistes N.I. Awards Music/Poetry Performance on Video

This Award is open to short films featuring music or poetry.
Each film is to last for a maximum of 3 minutes.

To facilitate this Award, Studio NI made available its facilities and equipment for contestants. Access was provided to venues such as the Crescent Arts Centre in Belfast, and a list of Public Domain songs and poems was put on-line for contestants who wished to participate in the Movie-Oke program.

A recommended book of poetry is "Other Mens' Flowers", edited by AP Wavell (while he was serving as a Field Marshall in the British Army during WWII). Other public domain poems have been included in the following pages of this book, so readers who are interested in the contributions to the TITANIA contests can get a feel for the poetry section entries.

'If—' by Rudyard Kipling
(TITANIA 2013 entry performed by Chris Heath)

If you can keep your head when all about you
Are losing theirs and blaming it on you;
If you can trust yourself when all men doubt you,
But make allowance for their doubting too:
If you can wait and not be tired by waiting,
Or being lied about, don't deal in lies,
Or being hated don't give way to hating,
And yet don't look too good, nor talk too wise;

If you can dream—and not make dreams your master;
If you can think—and not make thoughts your aim,
If you can meet with Triumph and Disaster
And treat those two impostors just the same:
If you can bear to hear the truth you've spoken
Twisted by knaves to make a trap for fools,
Or watch the things you gave your life to, broken,
And stoop and build 'em up with worn-out tools;

"Skeletons In The Closet"

If you can make one heap of all your winnings
And risk it on one turn of pitch-and-toss,
And lose, and start again at your beginnings
And never breathe a word about your loss:
If you can force your heart and nerve and sinew
To serve your turn long after they are gone,
And so hold on when there is nothing in you
Except the Will which says to them: 'Hold on!'

If you can talk with crowds and keep your virtue,
Or walk with Kings—nor lose the common touch,
If neither foes nor loving friends can hurt you,
If all men count with you, but none too much:
If you can fill the unforgiving minute
With sixty seconds' worth of distance run,
Yours is the Earth and everything that's in it,
And—which is more—you'll be a Man, my son!

JABBERWOCKY by Lewis Carroll
(TITANIA 2013 entry performed by Colin Dardis)

`Twas brillig, and the slithy toves
  Did gyre and gimble in the wabe:
All mimsy were the borogoves,
  And the mome raths outgrabe.

"Beware the Jabberwock, my son!
  The jaws that bite, the claws that catch!
Beware the Jubjub bird, and shun
  The frumious Bandersnatch!"

He took his vorpal sword in hand:
  Long time the manxome foe he sought --
So rested he by the Tumtum tree,
  And stood awhile in thought.

And, as in uffish thought he stood,
  The Jabberwock, with eyes of flame,
Came whiffling through the tulgey wood,
  And burbled as it came!

One, two! One, two! And through and through
  The vorpal blade went snicker-snack!
He left it dead, and with its head
  He went galumphing back.

"And, has thou slain the Jabberwock?
  Come to my arms, my beamish boy!
O frabjous day! Callooh! Callay!'
  He chortled in his joy.

`Twas brillig, and the slithy toves
  Did gyre and gimble in the wabe;
All mimsy were the borogoves,
  And the mome raths outgrabe.

'Helas!' by Oscar Wilde
(TITANIA 2013 entry performed by Peter Quigley)

To drift with every passion till my soul
Is a stringed lute on which all winds can play,
Is it for this that I have given away
Mine ancient wisdom, and austere control?
Methinks my life is a twice-written scroll
Scrawled over on some boyish holiday
With idle songs for pipe and virelay,
Which do but mar the secret of the whole.
Surely there was a time I might have trod
The sunlit heights, and from life's dissonance
Struck one clear chord to reach the ears of God:
Is that time dead? lo! with a little rod
I did but touch the honey of romance —
And must I lose a soul's inheritance?

TITANS OF ULSTER WRITING AND MEDIA FESTIVAL

SATURDAY 23RD NOVEMBER 2013
HOLIDAY INN, BELFAST

- PROJECT TITANIA SHORT FILM CONTEST
- 50TH ANNIVERSARY OF DR WHO
- Action Cancer CHARITY RAFFLE
- 50 YEARS COMMEMORATION OF C.S. LEWIS
- CSI: TRUTH OR SCIENCE FICTION?
- NI NOVEL WRITING MONTH
- MEDIEVAL HISTORY OR HOLLYWOOD MYTH?

£5 TO BOOK ONLINE OR £8 ON THE DAY
WWW.TITANFEST.COM

LOTTERY FUNDED | arts council

Studio-NI.ORG
Northern Ireland's Largest Arts & Culture Group

Action cancer
Saving Lives Supporting People

Studio NI is dedicated to developing local talent. TitanFest is Northern Ireland's talent under one roof. This includes a series of Masterclasses in story-telling skills, both written and visual.
As TitanFest is held in November, it is part of Northern Ireland Novel-Writing Month (NINoWriMo for short).

The climax of TitanFest is the annual awards ceremony for the Top Independent Talented Artistes N.I. Awards
- or "TITANIAs" for short.

Studio NI Code of Behaviour
Anyone who attends a Studio NI event is expected to follow this Code for the entire duration of the event, including any informal pre- or post-event activities.
Studio NI reserves the right to amend these rules at any time without prior or posted notice and reserves the sole right of interpretation.

Studio NI members should treat each other with respect at events.

Studio NI reserves the right to revoke membership from and eject anyone at any time from a Studio NI event without a refund.

All Event Attendees must wear their membership badges at all times.

Please follow any and all rules set by the Event Venue management.

Personal belongings are brought at Attendees own risk.

Offering for sale of any merchandise at the event may be undertaken only in designated spaces with permission from Studio NI.

Press members at Studio NI events must display an official Studio NI Press Badge or be accompanied by Studio NI staff at all times.

All guests appear subject to work commitments. Panels and events may be cancelled or rescheduled due to unforeseen circumstances.

No refunds will be possible, except under extenuating circumstances and at the discretion of the Studio NI committee.

Page	Contents
1	Cover
2	About the Event
3	Index
4	Friday 22nd November 2013
5	Saturday 23rd November 2013
6	Top Independent Talented Artistes NI Awards
7	List of Contest Entries
8	Sunday 24th November 2013
9	Monday 25th November 2013
10	Sponsors
11	Schedule
12	Rear Cover

What car-parking facilities are available for the Saturday event at Holiday Inn, Belfast?

Attendees may use the NCP car park on the Dublin road - parking chips can be validated at Holiday inn reception desk, giving a fixed rate of £4.50 on Saturdays. They can also ticket on the street at £1.40 per hour until 6pm.

What accommodation is available for attendees at the Holiday Inn, Belfast?

The Hotel has reserved a block of rooms at a conference rate of £99 B&B per room. To book, ring in and book the rooms on (00 44) 02890 271706 quoting "Studio NI". Any rooms that have not been claimed by the 1st of November will be released.

Friday

50 Years Commemoration of the death of CS Lewis

Holiday Inn, Belfast

Time: 7.30pm-11.00pm

To celebrate the 50th anniversary of the death of CS Lewis, we have arranged an evening of book-readings with local SF&F novelists. Authors Lynda Collins, Philip Henry and Roslyn Fuller will be in attendance, with a variety of different works.

Since Studio NI is a society open to all creatives, attendees will also be given the opportunity to participate by reading their own work.

Saturday

NI Novel-Writing Month

Holiday Inn, Belfast

Time: 10:00-18:00

Studio NI hosts NI Novel-Writing Month every November, in conjunction with local writers like the Belfast Writers Group. The challenge is to write a 50,000 word novel in 30 days, starting on 1st November. At TitanFest, contestants will be provided with space for a *write-in* where they can work on their word count.

Any NI Novel-Writing Month contestants who complete the challenge by 6pm on Sunday night will be presented with their NaNoWriMo certificates at the prize-giving ceremony.

Writing Workshop

Holiday Inn, Belfast

Our experienced local writers will instruct the participants in the processes of generating ideas and converting them into well-structured stories. This is a fun and informal, group based, session designed to defeat *Writers Block* and Kick Start the creative process. The guests will also be happy to take questions on the highs and lows of writing for fun and profit.

Film-Making Question and Answer Session
Holiday Inn, Belfast
Find out how to become an award-winning storyteller from the best in the business. You'll hear how they manage talent, create the most engaging work and turn brilliant ideas into award-winning projects. You'll also get an expert's perspective on what they think a good storyteller should be and how their careers have evolved thanks to the people the audience never know about. Whether you work in the BBC, commercially or for independent producers, this is your chance to help develop your career and pick their brains.

Historical Realism in Fiction
Holiday Inn, Belfast
Dr Steve Flanders from Queens University Belfast will give us a talk on realism (or lack thereof) in Hollywood films such as Kingdom of Heaven, Robin Hood (2009) and Monty Python and the Holy Grail .

CSI Effect: Science Facts or Science Fiction?
Holiday Inn, Belfast
Real-life CSI: We reveal modern-day 21st-Century scientific techniques, and contrast them with historical methods of crime-solving as used 100 years ago by Sir Bernard Spilsbury, a contemporary of Sir Arthur Conan Doyle and a founder of forensic pathology.

Amanda McKittrick Ros: the world's worst writer?
Holiday Inn, Belfast
Amanda McKittrick Ros, from County Down in Northern Ireland, ranks as one of the worst writers of all time. We'll compare her work to that of others such as the infamous Scotsman William McGonagall, and the famous fantasy fiction The Eye of Argon. The audience will be left to choose, who truly was the world's worst writer?

50th Anniversary of Dr Who
Holiday Inn, Belfast
Time: 20:00 - 21:30
This is possibly the most-awaited event of the year. The last half-century has seen the creation of one of the most enduring Science Fiction franchises of all time. The Anniversary Special has been crafted to encompass the full history of the show. This is your opportunity to meet with fellow fans and to experience the Anniversary together!

TITANIA: Top Independent Talented Artistes N.I. Awards

There are four awards that will be presented at TitanFest, at 6.30pm on Sunday evening.

1) Masquerade Parade (Costume and Make-Up)

The Masquerade contest will be conducted at TitanFest, at 3pm on Sunday afternoon. Starting at Verbal Arts Centre, the parade will follow the full length of the walls of Derry

Join the horde as they make the full circuit of the Walls of Derry - in aid of Action Cancer! The walled City of Culture will face an incursion of heroes, villains and the undead. This City withstood the sieges of 1649 and 1689 - will it fall to the monsters of the silver screen? All proceeds to Action Cancer.

This is a showcase of Medieval and Fantasy costume-making for stage and screen. Local designers and costume-makers will have the opportunity to display their creations in a contest. The Guest of Honour and other artistes will select the winner.

2) Film-making

This Award is open to short films on a specific annual theme.
Each film is to last for 3-6 minutes.
Casting and Crew-Call announcements must be made through Studio NI, to enable maximum access for local talent to participate
The theme for 2013 is *"Skeletons in the Closet"*.

The shortlisted entries will be shown at TitanFest, at 7pm on Saturday evening, and on Sunday afternoon in association with the Foyle Film festival. The winner will be chosen by audience selection.

3) Music/Poetry Performance on Video

This Award is open to short films featuring music or poetry.
Each film is to last for a maximum of 3 minutes.

The shortlisted entries will be shown at TitanFest, at 7pm on Saturday evening, and on Sunday afternoon in association with the Foyle Film festival. The winner will be chosen by audience selection.

TITANIA: Top Independent Talented Artistes N.I. Awards

4) Writing

This is for short stories on a specific annual theme.
Each story is to last for 3-5,000 words.

The shortlisted entries are included in the annual Anthology collated by the Belfast Writers' Group, published by The ORB to raise funds for Studio NI's Curing Cancer campaign. For every copy sold, £1 goes to Action Cancer.

The Anthology for 2012-13 is "Ghosts in the Glass".

Entries for the Writing Award (2012-3) are:
1) Harland & Wolf — Philip Henry
2) Care For a Peek? — M. Rush
3) The Old Red Doors — Holly Ferres
4) The Ghosts in the Glass — Lynda Collins
5) Any Given Friday — Logan Bruce
6) Our Silent Guest — Sarah McNeill
7) Dancing in the Dark — John-Henry Parker
8) Peace of Mind — Phil Deane
9) Arthur Grey: Lucifer's factory — M. Rush
10) The Shifter — Neill W.G. Stringer
11) Two's a Crowd — Sarah McNeill
12) Thin Air — Holly Ferres
13) Sleeping in the Light — James Donnelly
14) Strangers on a Strange Train — Logan Bruce
15) Pictures of Lilly — Lynda Collins

Sunday
Train from Belfast to Londonderry, UK City of Culture
Europa Train Station, Belfast
Time: 09:15
Our special Sunday event starts with a tour passing various locations used in filming, including Game of Thrones Season Two. The tour begins at 09.15 am departing from the Europa train station in Belfast. The Derry train passes under Mussendon temple, then along Downhill Beach - AKA Dragonstone, where King Stannis burned the Seven Gods of Westeros.

When we arrive at the Train Station we are transported by shuttle-bus to the bus depot. Then we begin a Walking Tour of the Walls of Derry, as far as the Verbal Arts Centre. This will allow GOT fans to get a taste of a real-life King's Landing, and tour the walls of a city that was violently besieged for months on end.

Bacon Buttie Brunch Hot food served at Verbal Arts Centre
Time: 11:30 - 12 noon
To be served on the Attendees' arrival at Verbal Arts Centre: soup and bacon baps (and a vegan option suitable for vegetarians and people with other dietary restrictions) with tea and coffee

Melee combat workshop
Great Bastion on the Walls of Derry
Our Fencing Masters, Mike and Lukasz, will conduct a fighting demonstration on the Great Bastion on the Walls of Derry.

Afterwards, attendees will be allowed to participate in a training session - safe fencing equipment will be supplied.

Talk to a Publisher (Lagan Press)
A professional publisher from Lagan Press, will deliver a list of Dos and Don't for aspiring authors, as well as offering himself for a Q&A session.

Medieval Victory Banquet feast
Hot food served at Verbal Arts Centre
Time: 18:00
pork roast/chicken (and a vegan option suitable for vegetarians and people with other dietary restrictions) with wine and orange squash

Train from Londonderry to Belfast
Londonderry Translink Station
Time: 19:00
When we arrive at the bus depot we are transported by shuttle-bus to the Train Station.
The Derry train passes along Downhill Beach (where King Stannis burned the Seven Gods of Westeros), then under Mussendon temple.

Monday
Dead Dog Party
Holiday Inn, Belfast
Time: 12:00 noon
The Dead Dog Party (known to the organisers as the TGIO or Thank God It's Over Party) is the final event of the weekend. Everyone who is still in town can drop by for a drink and a bite to eat. This is another opportunity to meet and socialise with the other attendees, your fellow creatives. If you are lucky, a few of the guests might even drop in for a drink or two!

LOTTERY FUNDED

Studio-NI.ORG
Northern Ireland's Largest
Arts & Culture Group

Action cancer
Saving Lives Supporting People

arts council of Northern Ireland
LOTTERY FUNDED

Studio-NI.ORG
Northern Ireland's Largest
Arts & Culture Group

Action cancer
Saving Lives Supporting People

Waterstone's

·THE·
BLACK
-STAFF
PRESS

·No Alibis

Holiday Inn

Friday		Cost	Number reqd
19:00	Registration	£5 annual fee	
20:00	Book Reading	Registration fee	
Saturday			
09:30	Doors Open	Registration fee	
09:50	Opening	Registration fee	
10:00		Registration fee	
11:00		Registration fee	
12:00		Registration fee	
13:00	Lunch	PAYG	
14:00		Registration fee	
15:00		Registration fee	
16:00		Registration fee	
17:00	Autographs	PAYG	
18:00	Dinner	PAYG	
19:00	Short Films	Registration fee	
20:00	Dr Who	Registration fee	
Sunday			
09:20:00	Train	PAYG (£7 retn)	
11:30:00	Walking Tour	Free	
12:00:00	NINoWriMo	Free	
	Masquerade	£5 Donation	
18:00:00	Dinner	£15.00	
18:30:00	Presentation	Free	
19:30:00	Train	PAYG (£7 retn)	
Monday			
	Dead Dog	PYG	

TITANS OF ULSTER WRITING AND MEDIA FESTIVAL

SUNDAY 24TH NOVEMBER 2013
VERBAL ARTS CENTRE
LEGENDERRY

- TOUR THE BATTLE-HARDENED SIEGE WALLS
- NI NOWRIMO WRITE-IN SESSIONS
- VICTORY BANQUET AT VERBAL ARTS CENTRE
- SMALL PUBLISHING IN NORTHERN IRELAND
- SWORD FIGHTING DEMO
- FOYLE FILM FESTIVAL
- MASQUERADE PARADE
- LITERARY DERRY: WALKING TOUR

£5 TO BOOK ONLINE OR £8 ON THE DAY
WWW.TITANFEST.COM

LOTTERY FUNDED | arts council of Northern Ireland | Studio-NI.ORG Northern Ireland's Largest Arts & Culture Group | Action cancer Saving Lives Supporting People

Proceeds to Charity!
The Belfast Writers Present

Ghosts in the Glass & Other Stories
Edited by
Lynda Collins

BWG presents a collection of sixteen tales of the supernatural, featuring ghosts, fiends, and an assortment of monstrosities. This anthology will terrify and tease you with its feast of short stories full of fear, humour and suspense; raising the hairs on the back of your neck whilst raising money for Studio NI's chosen charity, Action Cancer.

Join Katy on work experience with her strange Uncle Arthur as they investigate the terrifying happenings at the old Lucifer factory, or newspaper reporter Harland McNeill, who bites off more than he can chew when he teams up with two brothers who have their own strange brand of justice when it comes to investigating a spate of xenophobic murders.

Featuring stories by Philip Henry, M.Rush, Holly Ferres, Lynda Collins, Logan Bruce, Sarah McNeill, John-Henry Parker, Philip Deane, Neill W.G. Stringer, James Donnelly and Peter Gallagher.

Ghosts in the Glass and other stories is a collection of tales that will haunt you long after you put the light out.

Copies can be ordered on-line from
http://orb-store.com/ghosts.htm

Lightning Source UK Ltd.
Milton Keynes UK
UKOW04f0855271113

221931UK00001B/22/P

9 781907 572036